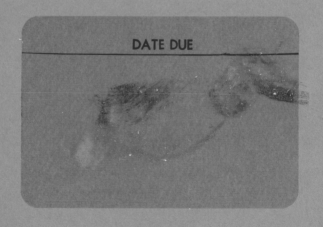

DATE DUE

NUTTY, THE MOVIE STAR

Dean Hughes

ATHENEUM   1989   NEW YORK

Atheneum
Macmillan Publishing Company
866 Third Avenue, New York, NY 10022
Collier Macmillan Canada, Inc.
First Edition   Designed by Eliza Green
Printed in the United States of America

1 2 3 4 5 6 7 8 9 10

Library of Congress Cataloging-in-Publication Data
Hughes, Dean.
Nutty, the movie star/by Dean Hughes.
—1st ed.   p.   cm.
Summary: Eleven-year-old Nutty, hoping to improve his image with his fellow
fifth graders, finds his popularity unexpectedly boosted when he gets a small
part in a Hollywood movie.
   ISBN 0–689–31509–0
   [1. Schools—Fiction. 2. Popularity—Fiction. 3. Actors and actresses—Fiction.
4. Humorous stories.] I. Title.
PZ.H87312Nw   1989   [Fic]—dc19   88–36614   CIP   AC

*For Richard
and
Joan Kendell*

Chapter 1

Nutty was the last one to poke his head into the darkness. He couldn't see a thing. But up he went. He moved slowly, being careful not to make a sound, and once he had pulled himself all the way up into the crawl space and onto the ramp, he felt his way forward, inching along on all fours. When his hand touched Orlando's shoe, he knew he had caught up with the others. "Okay, go ahead," he whispered.

Slowly, silently, the boys edged ahead. They had done this three times in the last couple of weeks, so they knew the procedure. The idea was to crawl about thirty feet until they were above the classroom next to the custodian's closet, where they had entered the crawl space. From above the false ceiling, they would be able to hear what the girls down below were saying.

Bilbo, who was first in line, stopped a little too soon. Nutty couldn't hear very clearly. He reached out and tapped Orlando on the behind. But Orlando apparently didn't understand the message. He threw out a little mule kick that barely missed Nutty's nose. "Watch it," Nutty whispered. "Move up a little."

But Nutty heard a voice below say, "What was that?" All the boys froze.

The girls didn't seem too concerned, however. They were quiet only for a few seconds, and then they returned to their conversation. Finally, Nutty reached up and flipped Orlando on the backside again, and this time Orlando apparently sent the message forward—through Richie to Bilbo. The boys moved ahead.

Nutty could now hear one of the fifth-grade girls—it sounded like Carrie—complaining that her father had packed a tuna sandwich for her again. The girls were the pickiest eaters Nutty had ever seen. They hated the cafeteria food, so they all brought their own lunches, but they didn't like those either. Of course, Nutty was a little sensitive on this issue. Everyone kept reminding him that he had promised, way back when he was elected student council president, that he would do something to improve school lunches. And they weren't seeing any change. In fact, something of a protest was going on these days. About half the kids in the school were bringing their own lunches—a way of telling Dr. Dunlop, principal of the university laboratory school, what they thought of the meals in the cafeteria.

The fifth-grade girls all ate in Mrs. Smiley's classroom. They claimed they were protesting, the same as the rest, but Nutty thought they especially liked to eat in private, so they could talk. It was that theory, in fact, that had inspired the boys to climb into the crawl space and listen. And they hadn't been wrong; they had already heard some juicy stuff.

"But he's not just cute," Nutty heard a girl say. "He's really nice, too, and he's smart."

Nutty recognized April's voice, and he smiled. He was sure she was talking about him. She had had a crush on Nutty since about third grade. All the same, it was kind of embarrassing for the other boys to hear her saying things like that.

"He's so tall and so strong, but his voice is really soft. I think he's kind of shy."

That was Carrie. Nutty had no idea she liked him, too. But then, he wasn't exactly surprised. He was pretty tall and a good athlete. He'd never thought of himself as all that strong, but maybe girls thought so.

"What I can't believe is the way he looks at me. He's got those dark eyes and those long eyelashes. When he smiles, I get goose bumps all over."

Abbie, too? Nutty was amazed. But what was this about dark eyes? He didn't have dark eyes. She must mean dark blue.

"Oh, I know. And don't you love his name? It sounds like a movie star's."

Mindy must be losing her mind. Nutty Nutsell was not a movie star's name. Freddie Nutsell wasn't any better. When girls fell for a guy, they were really sort of ridiculous. Nutty knew he was probably pretty good looking, but he really wasn't all that incredible. And the amazing thing was, Mindy had always pretended she couldn't stand him.

3

"I know. Lance Knight. It sounds like the hero's name in one of those old-fashioned movies."

What? Wait a minute. All this stuff was about this Lance guy?

Nutty couldn't believe it. Lance was a new guy who had just moved in that week. Sure he was tall, and maybe he was good looking—Nutty hadn't thought about that—but he was nothing to get excited about. Lance Knight. What a stupid name.

"Lance Knight. It gives me chills to say it. If he would like me, I wouldn't care if one other good thing ever happened to me in my whole life."

Nutty couldn't believe this stuff. Zoie had said the same thing about one of the sixth-grade guys just last week. What was it with girls? Some guy moves in, and suddenly the whole fifth grade has to fall in love with him. That was the worst thing about being in a lab school—the school was so small that a new kid always seemed like a big deal. But it wouldn't last. The guy was not that . . .

"He'll be elected student council president next year for sure," Mindy said.

"I know. He'll be twice as good as Nutty."

This time Orlando's kick was only playful, not hard, but it clipped Nutty's forehead, and someone up front in the crawl space let out a little giggle. Nutty was pretty sure it was Richie, not Bilbo. The guy was going to get it when they got down.

"Nutty never has kept his promises. He said we'd start getting hamburgers for lunch and pizza and stuff like that."

4

Nutty knew that voice. Ami. She always had been a negative person. She could criticize, but she didn't know....

"I know. He talks big, but he's scared of Dr. Dunlop. If William Bilks didn't help him, he'd never do anything."

"I don't think he's been that bad."

Nutty knew that voice for sure. And he liked it. It was Sarah Montag, his...well, anyway, it was Sarah Montag.

"Sure, Sarah, you just say that because you like Nutty, and he likes you." Nutty knew the voice; it was Abbie.

"Yeah, Sarah, if Lance asked you to go with him, you'd forget about Nutty in five seconds. And you'd admit he hasn't been a good president."

"He's done okay. No one else would've done any better."

"Lance would," Abbie said.

Well, Abbie, Nutty said to himself, you be his campaign manager then. And get married to him while you're at it. What do I care?

Nutty stared ahead in the darkness. He was almost sure he had heard one of the guys snickering again.

"Nutty tries to act like he's serious about things, but he's really not. He's just the same old Nutty that he's always been."

If only Nutty were down there. He could tell April a thing or two....

"They speak the truth," Orlando whispered. He had apparently sat up and twisted around, and then, for

emphasis, he reached back and gave Nutty a little cuff with his hand.

"Orlando, you're going to get it. When we get down, I'm going to—"

"Ssshhhhhhhhh."

Nutty knew he did have to be quiet. He could hear the other two guys laughing, too. He decided they all better leave before they got caught. He gave Orlando's foot a little yank and then started backing up. What he really wanted to do was dive right through that false ceiling and then tell a few girls what he thought of them.

"Nutty was better than any of the other guys in our class would have been."

Nutty stopped.

"That's not saying much. We should have elected Angela. She would have been better than any of the stupid boys."

"Yeah, Bilbo just reads all the time. He would have forgotten to go to the student council meetings."

"And Richie wouldn't have cared what happened. He never has an opinion about anything."

"Then there's Orlando. He always has an opinion—whether he knows anything about the subject or not."

"Yeah, Orlando would have spent the whole time telling how great he was. He's cocky enough without being president."

Nutty reached out and rapped Orlando a pretty good one and then put his head down to muffle his laughter. He just couldn't help it.

6

Orlando was backing up now, his shoes pushing into Nutty's arms. Nutty started moving back, maybe a little too quickly.

"What's that?" one of the girls said. "I heard something."

The four boys turned into statues again.

"It sounds like rats in the ceiling."

"Oh, don't say that."

The girls were quiet for a time, apparently listening. The boys didn't move. But before long one of the girls said, "I didn't hear anything," and they started talking again. Nutty took the chance to move back, very slowly, until he got to the access opening. He reached down with his foot, found a step on the ladder, and then climbed down to the floor.

He waited, and soon Orlando's feet appeared. When all three boys had climbed down, they quickly set the ladder against the wall, where they had gotten it. They weren't safe quite yet, however. They were in the custodian's little supply room, and they had to get out without being seen.

"Who do those girls think they are?" Nutty said, as much to himself as anyone else.

"They sure got you." Orlando laughed right out loud.

"Be quiet," Nutty said. "They got you worse."

"No way. All they said was that I'm cocky. But I've got a right to be cocky. What's your excuse?"

"I'm not as beautiful as Lance Knight—that's all. If you think I care about that, you're nuts."

"Well, I think you care about it, so I guess I'm nuts."

"I think you care, too," Bilbo whispered.

7

"So do I," Richie said. "That's my very strong opinion on the subject."

"Oh, lay off. All of you."

"At least Sarah still likes you," Orlando said in a sugar-sweet voice.

"Orlando, I'm going to pop that pimple that's sitting on top of your neck—if it ever comes to a head."

"What pimple? I don't have any pimples."

"Yeah, you just proved that."

"What?"

Nutty decided to ignore him. He flipped the light off and stepped to the door. Mr. Skinner always ate his own lunch during this time—in the cafeteria—so he wasn't likely to come along, but other kids could be in the hallway.

Nutty opened the door just a crack and then a little more when he didn't see anyone. He stepped out and looked both ways and then said quickly, "Okay. Hurry."

The other three boys stepped out, and they shut the door. They were safe. But they didn't have much time now if they wanted to get something to eat. They hurried down the hallway to their lockers and got their sack lunches.

They were heading outside when Zoie and April came out of the classroom where they had been eating. "So, Nutty," Zoie said, "you won't eat the lousy cafeteria food either. Why don't you do something to get it changed?"

"Hey, I've been trying all year. You don't know how hard it is to get Dunlop to do anything. He keeps promising, but he—"

"You don't have to tell us," April said. "We know about people who make a lot of promises they don't keep."

Were you born a little snot, or did someone train you? Nutty wondered, but he decided not to say it. He was just glad his term in office was almost over. He never wanted to run for anything again. Let someone else try, and let someone else take all the criticism. Maybe April would like to give it a shot.

Now the other girls were coming, all smiling, looking satisfied, as though they were glad they had just said such terrible things about him. Talk about heartless! Sarah stayed back, behind the others. Nutty wondered what she was thinking. His eyes met hers for a moment, but she quickly looked away.

"Nutty, the great president," Abbie said. "Can we have your autograph?"

Nutty turned to leave.

"Hey, what's that on your knees? Where have you guys been?"

Nutty glanced and noticed all the dust on his jeans. He reached down and brushed them off as best he could. So did the other guys. It was something they should have remembered from the times before.

"Have you little boys been playing marbles?" Mindy asked.

But Nutty and the guys were getting out of there.

"Some guys in fifth grade are too old for stuff like that. Some guys are tall and handsome—and even nice. They're not little boys, like some other fifth graders we know."

Mindy was going to get it someday. That girl never let up. Nutty and his friends just kept walking, but when they reached the doors, Mindy called behind them, "Some fifth-grade boys would make good presidents next year, and some already showed they can't do it."

Nutty kept his mouth shut, but Orlando spun around. "Oh, yeah? What about some fifth-grade girls who sit around and talk about—"

Bilbo grabbed Orlando and clapped a hand over his mouth. Then he pulled him out through the doors. Orlando struggled the whole way. He was furious.

But Nutty wasn't so much mad as he was worried. He didn't want everyone saying he had been a lousy president. He had to think of something he could do that would change some minds before his term was over.

The girls claimed he couldn't do anything without getting help from William. But that was stupid. He did lots of things without running to William.

All the same . . . he hadn't seen his old friend for a while. And if the subject did happen to come up, maybe they could chat a little. And—who knows?—maybe William would have some ideas. I don't need his help, Nutty told himself. I can handle this myself. But what could it hurt—just to get his thoughts on the subject?

Chapter 2

"Well, Nutty, I simply don't see the problem." William was leaning his chair backward on its rear legs, and he had his feet up on his bed. Of course, he had taken his shoes off first, and he had put them away in his closet. And he had put on a sweater, now that the evening was getting "just a tad cool."

"What do you mean, William?" Nutty said. "Everyone thinks I've been a lousy president. I didn't get any of the stuff done that we told them I was going to do."

"Yes, yes. I know that. But think about that. Presidents always promise things they don't deliver. And they are always criticized. That's just the nature of politics."

"William, this isn't politics. It's president of the student council, for crying out loud. And kids think that if you say you're going to do something you ought to do it."

"Well, of course. Children are a little more simplistic

11

about those sorts of things, but they are essentially the same as any human being. They complain a great deal, but they know they didn't really anticipate that you would accomplish anything when they elected you."

Nutty was lying on the floor. He had his hands behind his head, and he was staring up at the ceiling. He could see a little wisp of cobweb clinging to the light fixture. He was surprised that William hadn't spotted it by now. It was the only flaw in the otherwise perfect room. Everything William did was perfect—or very close. But he was finally showing that he didn't really understand kids his own age. But then, he had never been his own age, so maybe he had an excuse.

"William, what I want you to help me do is figure out some way to get Dr. Dunlop to start serving hamburgers and pizza and stuff, so everyone will say I did a good job."

"Fine. We can give that a try, but you have to understand that Dunlop's basic plan is very difficult to beat. Every time you bring the topic up, he says, 'We're looking into that, and we just might do something,' but that only stalls you off. He figures if he stalls long enough, the whole thing will go away. He's just about stalled it out to the end, so he's played things pretty smart."

"It's a dirty trick, if you ask me."

"Surely. But that's how the system works. It's like a president and Congress working together. They each play the game to their own advantage."

"Criminy, William, why do you always have to make things so complicated?"

"Oh, believe me, I'm not. You're the one who's complicating things. You're assuming that a good president has to keep his promises. I'm the one who's telling you not to worry about it."

Nutty started looking for more cobwebs. He thought maybe some had gotten into William's head. Nutty had never heard him say such stupid things.

"Here's the thing, Nutty. People always complain about their leaders, but either they like them or they don't like them. It has more to do with image than anything else. Some presidents are popular no matter how bad they are, and some are hated even if they do pretty well."

"Are you sure about that, William? Why would that happen?"

"Well, it's just the nature of people. Issues are too complicated, so people go by their emotions."

"Just tell me this. How do I get people to like me then? Or to say that I did a good job?"

William rocked his chair back and forth, like somebody's grandpa on the front porch. He nodded from time to time, as though he were agreeing with himself. Finally he said, "It seems to me that the fickle nature of your constituency has led to a momentary—"

"What?"

"Oh ... uh ... what I mean is, the voters—the children who put you in office—have become attracted to a new face. This fellow with the silly name ... Spear, or whatever it was ..."

"Lance. Lance Knight," Nutty said.

"Yes. This boy is apparently tall and attractive. He

may be stupid as a log, but the girls like his appearance—think he looks like a movie star."

"Actually, he's quite smart."

"Well, in any case, in politics a new face is always exciting for a while until everyone figures out that he's just another human like the rest of us. In the long run being smart usually works against a politician. Thoughtful statements are never as interesting as intense, truly believed, stupid ideas. Smart people have trouble saying that sort of thing."

Nutty rolled over onto his face, his nose smashed into William's shag carpet. "William, listen to me," he mumbled into the rug. "You are the age of a fifth grader, no matter how smart you are and what school you go to, and I am a fifth grader. We are not talking about the president of the United States. We are talking about the lab school and the student council." He took a deep breath through his mouth, since his nose was rather closed off for the moment. "I want to know what will make the kids think I'm better than Lance."

"So you want to be reelected. Is that it?" William asked.

"No."

"Of course you do. That's how politicians prove themselves. If you got yourself elected again, you would solve this ego problem you seem to be struggling with. You would know that everyone loves you after all. It's all a game of vanity."

"William, one last time. Only one. I just want to know what to do." Nutty rolled off his nose and onto his back again. If William didn't give him a straight answer, he was leaving—either that or committing murder. But William was thinking. That was a good sign—usually. Today it might only make things worse.

"All right," William said after a time. "Here's what I suggest. You must beat this Spike fellow at his own game. If the girls think he's a potential movie star, what you need to do is become an actual movie star. If you could get even a small part in a movie, you would suddenly have the entire school eating out of your hand—even if it was a cafeteria lunch." William chuckled to himself. He obviously liked his little joke.

But Nutty thought maybe William had finally gone off the deep end. "William, you may be smart, but you're saying some really dumb stuff today."

"Oh, really? For instance?" William asked.

"How could being a movie star have anything at all to do with being a good president?"

William chuckled all the more and for quite some time. He leaned back with his arms folded across his chest and came about as close as he ever had to an out-and-out laugh.

"Well, answer me."

"Nutty, I didn't say it made sense. I just said that's how it is. And what I'm trying to tell you is that you have to fight this guy's image with your image."

"But an image is just ... nothing. It's just words and ideas and stuff that aren't really real."

"Exactly," William said. "And you have to have more of that unreal stuff than he does, or you lose."

"I'm not running."

"Yes, of course you are. I'm going to do some research for a couple of days. I'll see what it takes to get you a movie part, somehow. And I'll read up on acting technique. We'll turn you into a movie actor, and poor Javelin won't have a chance. An image may be a lot of nothing, but real nothing always sells better than nothing nothing, if you get my drift."

Nutty got nothing from all this nothing other than getting out. He was not interested in becoming an actor. He decided to forget the whole thing and let the kids think what they wanted. He would give one last try at getting better lunches and then just be happy never to be a president again.

Nutty thought he had settled matters in his mind, but as he walked home, he noticed that something else kept sneaking into his thoughts. He kept remembering the things the girls had said. There was all that stuff about his not keeping his promises, but there was also something else. He had a feeling they just didn't take him seriously. Lance was some kind of dream boat, and a hero, and "nice" and everything else. Nutty was just...nutty.

When he got home, he found his mom in the living room. She was reading the newspaper. She said that Dad wasn't home, that he had to go to some kind of meeting.

"Mom, can I get your opinion about something?"

"Sure."

"Okay." But Nutty lost his nerve. "That's good to know. If I ever need to ask you something, I'll know you're willing to answer." He started to walk away.

"Come on, Freddie, what is it?" She put the paper down.

"Nothing. I was just—"

"There's something you wanted to ask me. Go ahead. You don't have to be embarrassed—no matter what it is."

"Well, I was just wondering... when I get older, say, and I start to be interested in girls... I'm not now at all, but I just mean when I get that way... what sort of... what do they... I mean... Oh, never mind."

"No, come on. What sort of what?"

"What sort of... guys... do you think they like?"

"Well, I think they get crushes on boys who are nice looking and athletic and all that. But I think when they get a little more serious, they like boys who also have some brains. And I think they like thoughtful, sensitive boys, who care about their feelings. I think those things become just as important as looks, once girls start growing up."

"So what are you trying to tell me—that I'm ugly?"

"No. What makes you say that?"

"Because it sounds like you're saying, Maybe you're not good-looking, but you can still get a girlfriend some day."

"No, not at all. Tall, slender, blond guys like you are just what girls are looking for. I'm just saying that that's not enough. Along with being handsome, I hope you'll also be kind and considerate. There's nothing wrong with a little tenderness in a man."

Nutty was standing in front of his mother, with his hands on his hips. "Are you sure it's still that way? Maybe it was just that way when you were young."

17

"That wasn't exactly a century ago, Freddie. I don't think those things change anyway."

"Maybe girls nowadays just like 'hunks,' whether or not they're sensitive or anything like that."

Mom laughed and said, "No, I don't think so."

Maybe she was right. He remembered what the girls had said about Lance—that he was nice and smart and everything.

"So what's going on? Does this have anything to do with Sarah?"

"Mom! I told you I don't like her. I don't like girls, period. See, that's why I don't like to ask you questions. You always jump to conclusions and start thinking...things."

She was smiling. "Right," she said, as if she thought she knew more about Nutty than Nutty knew about Nutty. That kind of stuff always drove him crazy. He decided to get out of there.

When he got away from Mom and went to his room, he did try to picture himself being like that—sensitive and kind and all that stuff—but he just couldn't imagine it. The only time he had ever been really nice to people was when his science project went crazy and the photons made him act so weird. The only thing that did was make everybody think he had turned into some kind of wimp.

How come girls said they wanted boys to be nice, but when guys acted that way they called them wimps? How come they said they wanted guys to be smart, but if they were—like William—they called them nerds? There was no way to win something like that.

He did remember what Sarah had said—that Nutty was not so bad. But that's all she had said. She would probably be in the Lance Knight fan club before long too. Or if he decided he liked her, she'd switch to him, just like the girls had said.

"I don't care," Nutty said aloud. And he made up his mind that that was the best way. Girls were too hard to figure out, and he didn't want a girlfriend anyway. He didn't need that kind of trouble. But he still kept remembering those girls making fun of him, talking about him as if he were a big loser.

Nutty thought for quite some time, but everything just kept going in circles. Finally he decided enough was enough. He got up and went looking for his little sister. Maybe he could bother her for a little while— add just a little misery to her life. It was something to do.

Chapter 3

The next morning at school Nutty came into class without speaking to anyone. He felt different about the girls after they had all made fun of him the day before, and he was still sort of miffed that his buddies had enjoyed it so much. He plunked himself down in his desk, stretched his long legs out in front of him, and slid down in his chair about as far as he could go.

Mrs. Smiley gave him one of those looks that said, "I don't like the way you're sitting, but I won't say anything—at least not until the bell rings."

Nutty found himself irritated. What difference did it make to her how he sat? And then Lance came in. The wind had been blowing outside, and his hair was a little messy. He ran his fingers through it, and it smoothed out. But it was still sort of loose and free, like the hair on male models in magazines. Nutty had a feeling Lance worked hard to get that look. When Lance walked past,

Nutty couldn't resist. "Don't worry about your hair, Lance," he said. "It's just perfect."

"What?" Lance stopped by Nutty's desk. "What did you say?"

"I said your hair is just beautiful."

Lance laughed. "Thanks, Nutty." He smiled.

This guy was too much. "In fact, you're pretty all over, Lance. You must have gotten up early to get yourself ready."

"What's going on?" Lance asked. He really seemed baffled. "What's this all about?"

"Never mind."

Lance shrugged. "Okay." He started to walk away, and then he stopped and said, "You look nice too." He laughed again, and every girl in the class laughed with him.

He made me look like a jerk, Nutty thought, and he's the real jerk. Can't these girls figure anything out?

Mindy turned around and said, "You're just jealous because you're not gorgeous, like Lance."

"Right, Mindy. And you're jealous of my dog because she's just a little bit more of a woofer than you are."

"Shut up, Nutty."

"Can you scratch your ear with your hind foot?"

"I hate you, Nutty."

"Break my heart."

Nutty hated the way she talked, with her lips all puckered up, as if she had eaten something sour. And she wore the cutest little outfits every day, all color coordinated. The girl was pure pain. So were all the girls.

Nutty tried to slide even farther down into his desk, but Mrs. Smiley saw him and said, "All right, Nutty, sit up now. It's time to get started."

"He's trying to hide," Mindy whispered. "He's ashamed to have anyone look at his ugly face."

Nutty sat up and leaned forward. He whispered, "Mindy, lay off, or I'm not going to play 'go fetch' with you anymore."

"Nutty, that's enough," Mrs. Smiley said.

Nutty was depressed all morning, and things didn't get better when lunch came. He and his friends got their lunches and went outside by the playground and sat on the grass.

"I don't want to listen to those stupid girls anymore," Nutty told them. "I'm not climbing up there again." He took a look in his sack. "Oh, barf. My mom made me an egg salad sandwich. She's getting back at me for asking her to make my lunches."

"My mom makes me make my own," Richie said.

But Nutty wasn't paying any attention. "I know what they're talking about anyway."

"Our moms?"

"No, Richie. Think. What was I talking about? I said I don't want to listen in on the girls anymore."

"You were also talking about egg salad—"

"I know what the girls are talking about anyway. They're talking about Lance—sweetheart Lance. What a wimp."

"He's really a pretty good guy," Bilbo said.

"What are you talking about?" Nutty dropped his sandwich back in his sack and started searching for something edible.

"Just what I said. There's nothing wrong with him."

"He's a pretty boy, Bilbo."

"Maybe the girls think so, but he can't help that."

Orlando said, "He's supposed to be a jock. I heard he's a good basketball player, and he's a good pitcher, too."

"No way," Nutty said. "I'll bet he spread that rumor himself." Nutty couldn't believe these guys would stand up for a guy like that. "Did you see how he was running his fingers through his hair when he came walking in this morning—like he thinks he's some model in a commercial or something?"

"All he did was brush his hair back," Orlando said. "You do that all the time."

"Hey, my hair falls in my eyes. He puts too much mousse on his to let that happen."

"No he doesn't," Richie said. "It would be stiff if he did that."

Actually, Nutty knew that. He just couldn't stand to hear this stuff. "The guy is a phony and a wimp, and he plays up to all the girls. Can't you guys see that?"

"Hey, Nutty," Orlando said, "you're the one who acted stupid this morning. He was pretty nice about it."

"Okay, fine. The guy is really nice. He's just so nice we all love him to death. You guys sound like the girls."

Nutty had found an apple and a couple of cookies. He tossed the sack—and the rest of his lunch—at a nearby garbage can, but he missed. The sack had no more than hit the ground when he heard a voice behind him. "I'll get it." Nutty twisted around and saw Lance, who walked over and picked up the sack and dropped it in the can. "Is it all right if I eat with you guys?" he asked.

"Sure," Orlando said. "Sit down. It's nice to have you join us." And then he looked over at Nutty and grinned. Nutty didn't think he was funny. But then, Nutty didn't think anything was funny today.

Lance sat down, crossed his legs, and looked into his lunch sack. "I ate the school lunch the first few days," he said. "But it's pretty bad." He looked at Nutty. "They tell me you're the student council president, Nutty. Didn't you make some sort of promise that you were going to improve the lunches?"

"That's not as easy as you think. Dr. Dunlop keeps stalling me off, no matter what I do."

"Yeah, well, I guess if you've done your best, that's all you can do."

Every time this guy said something, he seemed to stick some extra meaning between the lines. "What's that supposed to mean?" Nutty asked.

"What?"

"Do you think you could do any better?"

"I don't know." He looked surprised that Nutty would ask.

"Aren't you running for student council president next year?"

"I don't know. I really hadn't thought about it. Do you think I should?"

"Oh, I definitely think you should," Nutty said, trying to make sure Lance didn't miss the sarcasm.

Lance nodded, and he seemed to think it was over. "Well, maybe I could. Would you be willing to be my campaign manager if I do?"

Nutty couldn't believe this guy. He sounded like he meant it.

Nutty went to see William that afternoon. He was thinking maybe he would run for reelection next year after all. Maybe he would try to get into a movie—or whatever it would take.

William was glad that Nutty was changing his tune. William had found the name of a Hollywood agency that specialized in child actors, and he thought now would be as good a time as any to call.

"If I'm an actor, I don't want to be a wimp," Nutty said.

"Okay. Don't worry. That's not your image at all." William was dialing the number. "Nutty, go into the kitchen and pick up the other phone so you can hear this."

Nutty walked in and picked up the receiver, and then he sat down at the kitchen table. He heard a very deep voice from a man who sounded as if he weighed five hundred pounds. "Yeah. Milo Matthiesen here. What can I do for you?" the man was saying.

"Yes. My name is William Bilks. I have a client in the city of Warrensburg, Missouri. I think he's an incredible find, and I wanted to give your agency first chance to take him on." William was making his voice deep and full, trying to sound like an adult. He didn't have to try that hard.

The man laughed, his voice sounding as if it were in a cave. "Everybody's got a great find these days. What's the kid's shtick?"

"How do you mean, sir?" William asked.

"What's his gimmick? His angle? What makes him different from every other kid who wants to get in the movies?"

"Oh, I see. Well, he's a great talent, nice looking, and he can—"

"I got enough of those kind of kids. California's full of pretty kids with sunshine smiles and—"

"No, no. That's not what we have here at all."

"Okay, then, what's he got? I don't have all afternoon. Just tell me why I want this kid."

"Well, sir, he's no pretty boy. He's more of an All-American kid. You know . . . midwestern, down-to-earth, red-blooded."

"Is he a farm kid, or what?"

"No. He's more of a—"

"A farm kid might be pretty good. We get these calls for a kid to play a farmer's son or something of that kind, and I've got all these California surfer kids with blond hair and dark tans."

"Well, sir, he's from a small community. He's not directly a farmer, but he's grown up close to the earth, knows the language of the common people. He's the kind of young man who knows what it means to put in a day's work."

Come on, William, what's the deal? Nutty almost asked out loud. William made him sound like some kind of toilet bowl cleaner he was trying to sell. "Just stick him in and he works for you all day long."

"Is he a real hick or what?" the man asked.

"Oh, no. Not at all. He's a bright young man."

"Well, I don't know. I'm not getting any image here.

26

Do you know what I mean? Are you an agent yourself, or—"

"Yes, sir. I'm relatively new in the business, but I'm definitely an agent."

"Well, maybe you are, but you're not giving me anything I can sell. Do you see what I mean? I do want to get some kids from your part of the country if I can, but I gotta have something that grabs me—or I won't be able to push him."

"I know exactly where you're coming from. Let me describe my client to you. He's eleven years old, but he's tall for his age, athletic, earthy, solid. I'll give you an image: He looks like the sort of guy who wins the Olympic championship in, say, the decathlon and then gets up on the winner's pedestal and hears the "Star Spangled Banner," and big tears start to roll down his rugged cheeks. He's tough on the surface, but inside those blue eyes is a hint of tenderness—that little touch that makes the girls go weak in the knees."

"Yeah, okay. I like that. The earth stuff is good. And I like the schmaltzy, flag-waving stuff. That's something I can work with. What I'm gonna need is a picture portfolio. If the kid has the look you're talking about, I might be able to use him, but I gotta have some pictures first."

"He doesn't have much acting experience yet, but he—"

"That doesn't matter. We're selling image here. We'll let someone else teach him how to act."

"Well, fine. I'll get his portfolio to you right away."

"Good. Make sure he's got some shots in there with

a cornfield in the background or something of that kind—or maybe a flag waving in the breeze. Don't give me any of those leaning-on-the-elbow, hair-full-of-hairspray kinds of shots. No open collars with chains or anything like that. Put him in a work shirt maybe—blue denim."

"Right. I've got the idea."

"Okay. Give me your name and number, and what's the kid's name?"

William gave his own name and phone number, but he seemed to stall on Nutty's name. Finally he said, "His actual name is Nutsell. Freddie Nutsell."

"You gotta be kidding. How am I supposed to sell a kid with a name like that? Doesn't he have some other name he uses?"

"Well, he has . . . a nickname. But I don't think that would work so well. Maybe he needs a stage name."

"Sure he does. You should've worked that out long before now. He needs something basic, earthy—you know, a breadbasket, down-home kind of thing." The man paused. "How about something like . . . Farmer, Holmes, House. Yeah, House. What about Parker House? There's a name that will stick in someone's mind. It has the ring of home and hearth, bread and meat."

"It rolls right off the tongue," William said, and he chuckled.

The man laughed too. "There ya' go. Parker House. Let's try that. Get me some pictures. I get a call for a kid like this every now and then, and I'm stuck with all these kids who think the earth is sand on the California beaches. I think I can do something with this kid."

"Okay. Great. We'll be in touch."

"You got it, Will. Get back to me."

Nutty put the phone down. He couldn't believe any of this.

Close to the earth? The only dirt he got close to was under his fingernails.

But here came William striding into the kitchen. "All right. We're in business!" he said.

"William. That was a pack of lies. I'm no farmer. And I hate work. Dad says I'm the laziest kid he knows."

"Nutty, we're talking image—not reality. You've got to get that clear in your head."

"Get what clear? There's nothing there."

"You said it, Nutty. I didn't."

Chapter 4

William had some ideas, but Nutty wasn't excited about any of them. He wasn't sure he wanted to sink his life's savings into a portfolio of pictures, and he didn't know where they could borrow a horse for him to sit on or a tractor he could lean against. It was the hair coloring that he refused absolutely.

"No way, William. You're nuts. The guys at school would never let me live it down if I showed up with my hair dyed."

"But you heard what Mr. Matthiesen said. He's got too many blond guys."

"Then darken the pictures," Nutty said.

"Well, yeah, I thought of that, but if you get a part, you would have to make your hair come out like the pictures."

"Look, William, I don't care. I'm not dyeing my hair."

"Okay, okay. I'll talk to the photographer. We can probably fix up the pictures. But the day may come when you'll have to bite the bullet on this one—if you really do want to be in a movie."

What had Nutty gotten himself into this time? Just once William ought to be able to get a nice, medium-sized idea, instead of a giant, super-deluxe, way-over-board, now-I'm-in-trouble-again model.

But for the next few days William acted like a big-time movie agent, and he loved every minute of it. Nutty knew that William never went to movies, that he thought the whole Hollywood image was stupid, and that he cared nothing at all for the money he might make. What William liked was wheeling and dealing, running the show—pulling something off. As he explained to Nutty: "I suppose, ultimately, I think of myself as a scientist and something of a philosopher, but I simply can't resist the chance to try my hand at the practical world from time to time."

But Nutty knew there was a little more to it. William liked to take on adults and show that he could outsmart them, that he could operate in their world. And operate he did.

Nutty also thought he knew another operator. Everyone at school seemed to think Lance was the coolest guy who had ever come along. Mrs. Smiley was as bonkers over him as any of the fifth-grade girls, and Dr. Dunlop had already learned his name. The man had taken five years to learn Nutty's.

But Nutty wasn't buying it. This Lance guy was just a little too good to be true. He always said the right thing—and in that gentle voice of his. He knew how to flash his smile for the girls, but he also knew how to act sort of tough around the guys. As it turned out, he was a pretty fair athlete, which always went over well with the boys—and the girls—and he was probably as smart as Bilbo, which impressed everyone, too. Big deal. He was only pretending he wasn't cocky.

But what could Nutty do? He'd just have to wait until everyone figured the guy out. William had sent the pictures off, with a letter all about Parker House, the "genuine American." Nutty almost lost his lunch when he read the stuff William had written: "Parker has grown up on clean air, rich soil, and the unspoken love of a good day's work. He knows the simple pleasures of life in the breadbasket of our great nation. He eats meat and potatoes for supper and finds his sweetest joy in watching a brilliant sunset illuminate the plains or in feeling the tug of a fighting bass on the end of his fish line."

"William, I like pizza; I hate potatoes. And I've been fishing about twice in my whole life." But William was not interested in Nutty's opinion.

After another week Nutty told his friends that he thought the girls were starting to lose some of their excitement about Lance, now that they had gotten to know him a little. The guy was playing up to all of them, and it was getting obvious. They were starting to see through him.

Nutty's friends didn't think so. They thought every girl in the school was absolutely bananas over Lance—even the sixth graders. Nutty said it was time to find out, and so they decided, in spite of what Nutty had said before, to sneak into the crawl space again and hear what the girls were saying now.

As soon as the hall cleared, the boys slipped into Mr. Skinner's closet, Nutty going last and checking the hallway one last time. They were getting the technique down to a science.

Nutty wanted to go first this time, but the guys told him he was too noisy; he better stay back the farthest from the girls.

"What are you talking about?" Nutty said. "Orlando was making all the noise last time."

"Hey, no way," Orlando said. "You kept slapping me on the rear end. I just kicked you a couple of times."

"Yeah. Right in the head. Don't start doing stuff like that this time."

"Oh, excuse me. You just go right ahead and slap me all you want. I won't think of defending myself."

"Both of you be quiet," Bilbo said. He had started up the ladder, but he waited until Nutty and Orlando had stopped before he opened the door in the ceiling.

In a few minutes they were all up in the dark, crawling slowly ahead. Once they were close enough to hear what the girls were saying, Nutty was relieved. They were talking about some television show. And after that it was what kind of shoes they all liked. This was all very boring, but at least they weren't talking about Lance. Nutty was pretty sure his theory was right; the guy was coming on too strong, and the girls were getting tired of him.

"Lance sure has neat shoes," one girl said. "He said he bought them in New York. Can you believe that?"

"Oh, I know. He's been everywhere."

That was Mindy. Nutty knew how stupid she was. But the other girls knew better....

"His dad gets transferred all over. They've lived in Germany and in the Philippines or someplace like that and all over the country. I think that's why Lance is so mature. He's had a lot of experiences for a guy his age."

Nutty let his head drop to the ramp. He couldn't believe it. Sarah, of all people! Nutty made a little gag sound, and Orlando let out a muffled little laugh.

"I just worry that his dad might get transferred from here before too long. How long does he usually stay in one place?"

"He says it varies a lot. He does some sort of work for the air force, but he's not in the air force. Sometimes he stays in one place a couple of years or so and sometimes not very long at all. He told me... well, I better not tell you what he said."

"What do you mean, Sarah? What did he tell you?"

"Well, it's ... sort of personal."

"Personal? What do you mean? You didn't tell us anything about this."

"I know. I thought I shouldn't. It was just between the two of us."

Nutty was beginning to wonder why he had come up here.

"What? What?"

Nutty wanted to puke right on the false ceiling. This was unbelievable. How could Sarah fall for all that phony stuff?

"Well, okay, I'll tell you guys. But don't tell anyone else," Sarah said.

34

"We promise. Don't we?" They all started vowing and promising.

"Well, he looked at me with those eyes of his, and he said, 'I hope I stay here a long time,' and he kept looking at me, and then... he winked."

"Winked? Oh, Sarah, really?"

Mindy started chanting, "You've got him, Sarah. You've got him."

"What about Nutty?" someone was asking in the middle of all this. "Don't you like him anymore?"

"Forget Nutty," someone else said, maybe Zoie, but it wasn't Sarah.

"She's got them all," Mindy said, "but I don't know why she would want Nutty if she has Lance."

"Shut your mouth, Mindy," Nutty mumbled out loud.

"What was that?"

Silence.

Nutty felt the guys in front of him hold their breaths. He didn't bother. He was too disgusted.

"What was that? It sounded like someone said something—up in the ceiling?"

"It must have been out in the hallway."

But they still listened a little longer before they started talking again, and the subject was soon the same. Nutty felt Orlando's feet edging back toward him. He reached up and slapped Orlando to signal him to stop, but he kept coming. Nutty could hear some movement further up front, and he knew that all three were coming back, but Nutty wanted to stay. He wanted to hear what Sarah was going to say about him.

Orlando gave a shove against Nutty's arm with one of his feet, and Nutty pushed back. But then he slid sideways, grabbed a metal tie that held up the crawl ramp, and leaned out as far as he could. He got hold of Orlando's belt and pulled to signal that he could go on by.

Orlando edged backward, and Nutty was able to keep his balance all right with one knee barely on the ramp. Richie got by, too. But then Bilbo came through, and he was simply bigger than the other two. Nutty leaned out farther and was okay for a time, but then he felt his knee start to slip. He reached for Bilbo, tried to cling to him, and for a second seemed successful, but his knee was slipping ever so slowly. And then he was gone.

His leg broke through the tile, but for a moment the metal straps held. Nutty grabbed at anything he could get hold of. But his weight was too much, and in one mighty gust, a whole section of the false ceiling gave way. Nutty flailed, tried to grab for something solid, but straps were pulling loose, and suddenly he dropped through the ceiling, taking a huge hunk of it with him.

He was able to right himself enough to fall feet first and save himself from getting hurt, but he came tumbling down just a few feet from all the girls. They screamed in wild unison and scattered away in all directions. Nutty hit on his feet and then tumbled to a sitting position. The ceiling tile was all around him, and fragments continued to drop. For a few seconds everything was still. Nutty looked about, frantically. He thought of jumping and running, but he was still sort of stunned.

The girls were gradually regaining their composure.

Some of them were demanding to know what he had been doing up there. He watched them try to decide whether they were going to laugh at him or get angry. But Mindy made her decision quickly, and she pushed the others in the same direction.

"Nutty, I know what you were doing. You were up there listening to us. Weren't you?"

Nutty didn't answer. He was watching Sarah and hoping to see some hint of a smile.

"Weren't you?"

"No way." Nutty was trying desperately to think of some excuse. "I was trying to . . . help Mr. Skinner repair the air conditioner."

"Oh, yeah, right. Nutty, we don't have air-conditioning."

"Well, I was . . . " He gave up. He smiled, sheepishly, and hoped for a little understanding. "No wonder it's so hard to fix."

"That's stupid. You were listening to us. I know you were."

Nutty glanced over at Sarah again. She was being entirely noncommittal. Nutty decided he just wouldn't care about it. He was caught, and denying wouldn't do any good. He got up and brushed himself off.

"Are you okay?" Carrie asked.

"Yeah, I'm okay." Nutty walked toward the door. He was just starting to realize what a super mess he was in. He wondered what it would cost to repair the damage.

Some of the girls had begun to tell Nutty what they thought of him. The general opinion seemed to be that he was disgusting. He was an eavesdropper. He had listened in on a personal conversation. They just couldn't believe anyone could stoop so low.

"I didn't stoop," Nutty said, as he went out the door. "I fell." He tried to laugh but didn't have much success.

"I'm telling Dr. Dunlop," Mindy said.

"I had a feeling you would. But I'll tell you what: I'll save you the trouble."

Out the door Nutty went and on down the hallway. When he passed the custodian's closet, he said, "Sit tight for a minute or two," to the guys inside. And on he went to the principal's office. Pieces of ceiling tile were in his hair and on his shoulders. He didn't even bother to brush them away. What difference did it make? Dunlop was going to have him for lunch, and then he was going to call his parents...and then...it was going to be a very long day.

Chapter 5

When Nutty walked out of Dr. Dunlop's office, his friends were waiting. "What's he going to do to you?" Orlando asked.

Nutty was not in a great mood to talk. He headed toward his locker. The boys followed. "He doesn't know yet," he finally said. "He has to think it over."

"Do you have to pay for it?"

"Yeah."

"Did you tell him we were with you?" Richie wanted to know.

"No."

Nutty stopped in front of his locker and glanced around at the other guys. He could see that Richie was relieved, but Bilbo looked troubled. "You shouldn't have to take all the blame," he said. "Or have to pay for the whole thing."

"I was the one who wanted to stay up there when you guys wanted to leave. So it was my fault."

"Your parents are going to go through the roof, Nutty."

"Or at least the ceiling," Nutty said, and he tried to smile. Yet he didn't know why; he certainly wasn't seeing anything funny in all this.

But Orlando couldn't resist. He started to laugh. "That was some crash," he said. "First I heard this sort of whoosh—I guess when the ceiling gave way—and then stuff was crashing all over. I was just about to start down the ladder, but I froze. For a minute we thought you might be dead or something, and then we heard you talking. I wish I could have seen those girls when all of a sudden some guy comes flying in through the ceiling."

"They did look surprised," Nutty said, and now he really was smiling, whether he wanted to or not. He remembered the look on Mindy's face.

"What do you think it will cost?" Bilbo said, and suddenly reality returned.

"I don't know. Quite a bit. More than I've got. My dad's going to scream bloody murder."

It was that image—of Dad turning red and screaming—that filled Nutty's thoughts all afternoon. Mrs. Smiley took the whole class to the library while Mr. Skinner cleaned things up. Nutty offered to help, but Mr. Skinner told him to get out of his sight—forever. Eventually the class returned to the room, but Nutty kept looking up at the gaping hole in the ceiling, and the thought of his dad's reaction returned every time.

There was no pleasure left in thinking of Mindy's terrified face. Her current look was one of disgust, and it was directed at Nutty as often as possible all the rest of the day. Every chance she got, she whispered some little insult: "Do you peek in people's windows, too?" "I hope you heard who likes Sarah—and who Sarah likes now."

After school Nutty walked slowly to his locker. He was in no hurry to get home, but he wasn't in any mood to hang out with his friends either. He stuck all his stuff away and slammed the locker. As he turned away, however, he saw Sarah, who had just walked up to her locker a little way down from his. When she looked up at him, he looked away and started to walk past her.

"Nutty, that was a rotten thing to do," she said. But she didn't sound mad. In fact, she sounded as if she were teasing.

"I know," he said.

"And it wasn't the first time."

Nutty stopped and looked at her more carefully. She wasn't exactly smiling, but there was something playful in her look. "How do you know that?"

"I got thinking about it this afternoon. Last week we saw you guys in the hall, during lunch, and you all had dust on your knees. We heard something up in the ceiling that day, too. I think you guys have been crawling up there every day."

"No. Not every day."

"How many times?"

"Uh . . . well, five times."

"You must have heard a lot of stuff."

41

Nutty nodded. Now it seemed a pretty crumby thing to do—even though it hadn't seemed so at the time. He felt stupid. "We just did it for the heck of it." Nutty couldn't tell what she was thinking.

"Well, I think it was pretty low. I also think that if I ever had a chance to listen to you guys, I would probably do it." She hesitated and let that sink in. "I think Mindy would too—or any of the other girls." Now she was really smiling.

Nutty shrugged. "We don't talk about the same stuff," he said. He thought about the situation turned around. The girls would only hear the stupid stuff Orlando was always saying.

"So you heard everything we said about Lance, didn't you?"

"Yeah."

"Some of that stuff was just—"

But a piercing voice suddenly came shooting down the hallway, like an arrow. "Sarah, how can you talk to that creep?"

Nutty didn't have to look around. He knew it was Mindy. "See you later," he said to Sarah, and he walked away.

"Going off to eavesdrop on someone, Nutty?" Mindy called after him. "Don't get careless and land on your head next time."

Nutty didn't look back. He walked out of the school and on home. He knew his parents wouldn't be there for a little while, and he was thankful for a little time alone. But, as it turned out, he wasn't that lucky. His little sister got home a few minutes after he did, and she had heard the whole story—sort of.

"Nutty, I can't believe what you did. It's so embarrassing to have you for a brother." She had her hands on her hips and her nose in the air. The girl could be very irritating.

"Thanks, sweety," Nutty said. He bent over and kissed her on the top of her head before she could jump away.

"Quit that," Susie said. "Don't get your slobber on my hair." She brushed her hair back with her hand—the way Lance always did.

"What are kids saying I did anyway?" Nutty asked.

"You climbed down through the roof of the building and—"

"I did not."

"And then tried to peek into the girls' bathroom."

"Hey, no way. Who's saying that?"

"Everyone. And you jumped through the ceiling."

"I didn't jump through. I fell through. And it wasn't in the girls' room."

"Oh, good. You didn't jump through; you fell through. That's a lot better. What were you doing up there anyway?"

"None of your business," Nutty said, and he decided to end the conversation. He headed for his bedroom.

"You were peeking at girls."

Nutty stopped. "No, we weren't. We just thought it would be funny to hear what those girls were saying—and then I slipped and fell. That's all that happened."

"You're not going to be president anymore."

"How do you know?"

"That's what everyone is saying."

"And that makes you happy, right?"

"Well, you don't deserve to be president. You do too many dumb things."

"Susie, I just want to know one thing."

"What?"

"Do you love me?" He suddenly grabbed her and hoisted her up in his arms, squeezing tight.

"Stop it, you jerk. Stop it." Susie flailed and kicked, but Nutty had her gripped tight, and she couldn't get at him very easily. "You make me sick. Quit it. Just quit it."

"What's the matter? Don't you love me?"

Nutty found a certain pleasure in Susie's anger, but he probably couldn't have chosen worse timing. During all the racket Mrs. Nutsell had come in. She was right behind him when she said: "Freddie, stop it. After what you've done today, I would think you wouldn't be in such a playful mood."

Nutty put Susie down. "Jerk!" she yelled.

"That's enough, Susie. Freddie, I'm so upset right now that I better not talk to you. Go to your room, and when your father gets home, we'll get to the bottom of this whole thing."

And so Nutty had to sit around and wait for an hour or so. He wasn't sure what bottom they were going to get to, but he wished, in a way, that he could just get it over with. He knew that all the speeches and disgusted looks were going to be worse than any spanking ever was.

When the confrontation finally came, Dad started out by asking for an explanation, which he interrupted at least a hundred times. "I can't believe you would do such a thing," he kept saying. "It's so silly, so stupid, so pointless, so immature."

Who needs Mindy? Nutty thought. He could get all the insults he wanted at home.

"It was just . . . a joke or something. I just thought it would be fun."

"Fun? Is that what it turned out to be? It could cost several hundred dollars to get the ceiling fixed. Does that sound like fun to you? Where do you propose to get that kind of money—or do you expect dear ol' dad to bail you out again?"

"I've got some," Nutty said. "I'll pay you back the rest."

"Oh, yes. Believe me you will. You're going to learn to take responsibility sooner or later and find out that you just can't—"

"Freddie, the phone is for you." Somewhere back there the telephone had rung, and Mom had gone to the kitchen to answer it.

Nutty got up from the living-room chair he had sunk himself into, and he walked out to the kitchen. "Make it quick," Mr. Nutsell said. "We're not finished here."

Nutty glanced back to see his dad plunge his head into his hands. He knew this delay would only give him a little rest so that he could start all over again. It was going to be a long evening.

William was on the phone. Nutty was not really in the mood to talk to him, but his jaw dropped when he heard what William had to say. He was so stunned he didn't even ask many questions. He kept saying, "Okay, okay. Yeah, that sounds all right."

When he went back to the living room, he didn't sit down. Dad looked up and said, "You know, Freddie, among other things, I'm embarrassed and disappointed that a son of mine would be labeled a peeping Tom and a—"

"I didn't peep at anyone. I just listened."

"Well, son, that's eavesdropping, and it's sleazy behavior. It's beneath someone with the name of Nutsell. It makes me wonder what kind of person you are becoming. The expense is bad enough, but the—"

"I just took care of the expense."

"What?"

"I just got an offer for two thousand dollars to be in a movie."

Dad was stopped cold. He stared at Nutty as though he hadn't understood the words. Mom said, "A movie? What movie?"

"I don't know exactly. I only know the name: *Country Style*. It's going to be on television."

"Who was that on the phone?"

"William."

"What?"

It was time to start from the beginning. "See, William is sort of like my agent, and we decided to see if I could get in the movies, so he called this guy in Hollywood— a real agent—and told him about me. So this guy just called and said he had a part for me."

"What do you mean, 'told him about me'? You've never done any acting." This was Dad now. He had come back to life.

"I know. But William told him that I was a down-to-

46

earth kind of kid. I guess they needed someone like that."

"You're going to be in a movie?" Dad still looked doubtful.

"It's a movie that was all made, and someone decided one of the scenes had to be done all over again. They needed a kind of farm kid, and this guy thought of me."

"Where will they film it?" Mom asked. "I've heard a lot about disreputable producers."

"Out in California."

"When do you have to be there?" she asked.

"Next week."

"Will they pay for your flight and expenses and everything?" Dad wanted to know. He was still skeptical.

"Yeah, everything. And they're paying to have William fly with me. Plus, I get two thousand dollars."

"Or will William get it?" Dad had a tendency not to trust William.

"No. He just gets ten percent. Two hundred. I'll get eighteen hundred bucks. They offered fifteen hundred at first, and William talked them up, so he earned his money and then some. After I pay for the ceiling, I should still have at least a thousand left over."

"For college," Mom said, letting go of whatever worries she may have had.

But Dad was finally into the thing. Nutty saw the little calculator in his head starting to whir, saw his eyes getting bigger and bigger. "College? Honey, we could be talking something a whole lot bigger than college. If he makes good on this, he could hit the big

47

time. We could be talking big bucks here."

"William says the same thing," Nutty said. "He says I've got the right image."

"Of course you do. You're a good-looking kid, with that blond hair and all. You look just like one of those California kids that make all the money."

"Well, actually, I—"

"Don't you have to know how to act?" Mother said.

"Oh, honey, how tough can that be?" Dad answered for Nutty. "The directors and all those people will show him what to do. The main thing is that the girls all go for him—and I know they will." Dad walked over and put an arm around Nutty's shoulder. "The girls have got to go for you. You look a lot like me." He looked over at Mom and winked, but then he added, more seriously, "Son, I'm very proud of you."

"Yeah, well, I just hope I can do all right this time, so I get some more chances."

"Hey, don't worry about that. You're a Nutsell. I've always known you'd do something really big with your life."

Nutty glanced at Mom, who was starting to laugh. Nutty just shrugged. Lots of things seemed to be falling through ceilings today.

Chapter 6

William came over later that evening. "Good heavens," he said, as he stepped into Nutty's room, "your dad is certainly excited. He just told me he thought you were going to be a big star."

"Yeah, well, thank goodness. I had sort of a bad day. He could have been pretty mad at me." Nutty told William about the great crash.

William turned Nutty's chair away from the desk and sat down, and then he listened to the whole story. "Oh, Nutty, Nutty," he said at the conclusion. "You try your best to self-destruct, don't you? Sometimes it's not easy for me to keep you going. This makes reelection much more difficult."

"Reelection. I'm going to be lucky not to be booted out of office right now," Nutty said.

"Well, possibly. But Dunlop usually backs down if he thinks a fight is coming."

"What fight? I don't think my parents would—"

49

"No, of course not. I don't mean your parents. But there's nothing Dunlop hates more than a phone call from me. I suspect that if I mention the possibility of a lawsuit, he'll buckle under." William chuckled. "But let's cross that bridge when we come to it. For right now, we need to work on your appearance."

Nutty knew what was coming. "I don't look like my pictures, do I?"

"No. He got a request for a farm kid the same day he got our pictures. He had to come up with someone immediately, and there you were. But if you show up with blond hair and no muscles, I'm the one in trouble."

"You mean I have to get my hair dyed?"

"Well, yes, but I've given the whole thing some thought. We have one other problem. Around here we need to have you look like you're from California, and in California we need to have you look like you just wandered in off the farm."

Nutty rolled off his bed and sat on the floor with his elbows propped on his knees. "Wait a minute, William. You're going to have to explain this one to me."

"Okay." William tried to cross his legs and almost lost his balance, since his feet barely reached the floor. He dropped the whole idea and slid back in his chair, and then he took on his thoughtful look again. "They expect a young man from the country—strong, silent, maybe just a bit . . . slow, perhaps."

"William, you told him 'rugged' and 'all-American,' not stupid."

"I know. But he picked up more on that 'earth' stuff.

We probably need to crop your hair a little, dye it in earth tones, and pad your clothes enough to give you the look of a boy who could get a bale of hay off the ground."

"Pad my clothes?"

"Sure. A little something in the shoulders of a jacket, maybe something in the arms. I'm sure a tailor could fix you up. Once you get through this part, you can start exercising with weights, but we don't have time right now."

"William, I think you've gotten me into a mess again. No one's going to think I'm a farm kid." Nutty let himself slide down until he was flat on the carpet.

"Nutty, I'm not asking you to go back there with manure on your shoes. I'm just asking you to assume a role. That's what actors do. It's a wonderful opportunity, not a mess." William rubbed his chin, like a little philosopher. "But remember, our original goal was to improve your image around here. You can't show up at school looking like a kid from the sticks. You have to fit the image of the Hollywood star."

"Hey, I've been thinking about that. When I tell Mindy I'm going to be in a movie, she'll pass out. I mean it. She'll fall right down on the floor, out cold. And I'm going to love it."

"I thought it was the one named Sarah you had the crush on. Have you switched to Mindy already?"

"No way." Nutty sat up. "William, I don't have a crush on anybody. But I can't stand Mindy. She made a big deal out of my ... accident. She treated me like I'm some kind of scummy eavesdropper."

"I can't imagine why. You simply invaded her privacy. I don't know why that should bother her."

William's sarcasm brought Nutty back to reality. He had almost forgotten what everyone was saying about him now. "Will people forget about that ceiling thing now?"

"Listen, Nutty, you have an uphill battle. We got what we wanted: the movie part. But now we have to counteract all this negative publicity you've just gotten. We have to play this movie star image for all it's worth. Until just before you leave for California we might want to lighten your hair a little and give it that California wind-blown, sand-and-sea look. We need to get you some of those surfer shirts and some—"

"Surfer shirts?"

"Well, I don't know exactly. But you need sunglasses, a dark tan—as much as I'm opposed to the effects of ultraviolet rays—and some sort of clothes that look, you know, cool. White pants, I think. Don't they wear white pants and flowered shirts out there? I saw the Beach Boys dressed like that once."

"William, I'm not going to school in white pants."

"You may have to, Nutty. We're going to have to go to Kansas City and see a fashion consultant and a hair dresser. In the meantime don't say a word to Mindy or anyone else about the movie. We need to spring this with just the right timing to get maximum effect. I'm thinking an article in the local and Kansas City papers would be the best opening shot."

Nutty stared up at the ceiling. William was really getting into this. "William?"

"Yes."

"There's something I'm really scared about."

"What's that?"

"All this sounds pretty fun: telling kids I'm in a movie, taking a trip to California, getting a bunch of money. But there's one thing that just keeps scaring the heck out of me."

"You can't act."

"Right. What do we do about that?"

"Okay. That is, ultimately, my purpose in coming over tonight. I'm going to give you your first acting lesson."

Nutty sat up. "Do you know anything about acting?"

"Well, I didn't until today. But I got a book from the library earlier this evening, and I read through it, just quickly. I think I have the idea now."

"But we don't have much time."

"I know. Let's get started." William stood up. He put his hands on his hips, cocked his head a little to the side while he thought. "All right. Let's start with this. Think of yourself as a fish. You're in a little fishbowl all by yourself, and—"

"Wait a minute. What are you talking about?"

"I just want you to think yourself into a part. I want you to become a fish, imagine the feel of the water, the sense of the world you live in. I want you to think as a fish."

"William, when am I ever going to get a part like that? That's stupid."

"No, no," William said. "I'm not saying you'll ever play a fish. I'm just trying to get you to envision yourself

53

as something outside yourself. The book says it's help-ful to start with animals because you have to distance yourself so completely from a sense of self. Do you get the idea?"

"No."

"Well, trust me. Think as a fish. Use those powers of concentration we've worked on. Shut your eyes and let yourself float, and see what kind of world you see be-fore you. Get a sense of the tactile, the touch of the water against your fins."

Oh, brother, Nutty thought. My fins!

Nutty shut his eyes, but he really didn't want to do this.

"Okay, feel the water, feel the motion," William said. "What do you see?"

"Nothing. My eyes are shut."

"Come on, Nutty, try. Open and shut your mouth. Let the water filter through your gills."

Nutty opened his eyes. He was about to protest, but there was old William, eyes shut tight, his mouth rounded. He began to pop his lips open and shut. "William, you look like an idiot."

"Hey, look at a fish some time. But you're supposed to have your eyes shut. Come on, give it a try."

So Nutty gave it a shot. He didn't open and shut his mouth, but he did try to feel as if he were floating. He even let his arms float outward, as though he were in a swimming pool. "All right. Good. Now think your way into that world. What words would you say if you were a fish?"

"Criminy, William. That's stupid. Fish can't talk. They

54

just swim around and look for stuff to eat. 'Food. Food.' That's probably the only thing they think. 'Give me some more of that rotten-smelling stuff you guys sprinkle in my bowl.'"

"Okay," William said. "That's a start. You're getting a sense of 'fishness.' The purpose of life is to eat. But maybe a fish likes to drift with the current of the water, feel the pleasure of mere existence. Maybe—"

"I don't want to be a fish, William. That's not going to help me one bit next week when I have to do some real acting."

William looked disgusted. He let his breath out in a long stream. "Okay. Let's get right to human beings. But Nutty, try harder this time." William walked over and turned the chair around toward the desk, and he sat down. "Here's the situation. You're a farmer, and I'm your wife."

"I think I can find a better-looking wife on my own."

"Maybe not," William said, with a little smile. "Now shut your eyes, though, and don't think about me or about this room. Think of yourself as a farmer. You've been out working in the fields all day, and there's a drought. Your crops are burning up, and you feel like—"

"If my crops are burning up, what am I doing out working in the fields?"

"Okay. Right. Good thinking. Here's how things really are. Try to picture this." William hesitated but then began his description in a dramatic voice. "You can't work, and you wish you could. All you can do is wait for the rain to come, and you can hope. You've gone outside to look at your corn, and your heart is breaking.

Discouraged, downhearted, almost in despair, you come back to the house. Your wife is finishing her breakfast and is about to go off to work for the day. She's had to take a job to help make ends meet. You hate to see her go to work. Your pride is hurt. Now... try to get the feeling. Know the heart of that man as he comes tromping into the kitchen. Make your entrance and then speak as he would speak."

Nutty shut his eyes and tried to picture it all. "What's my wife having for breakfast?" he asked.

"I don't know, Nutty. What difference does it make? Mush, I guess."

"No. It's too hot. Maybe a boiled egg and some toast."

"Okay, fine. Egg and toast. Now... get yourself thoroughly into the part and enter the house."

"How soon does she have to leave?"

"Nutty, stop this. Just get on with it."

"Hey, you're the one who—"

"Okay, okay. Ten minutes. Now enter the house. Remember, you've never been so discouraged in your life."

Nutty took a few steps back and then he pretended to open a door and enter the kitchen. His shoulders suddenly dropped, as though he were imitating a great ape instead of a farmer, and his head hung almost to his chest. He stomped slowly over to William.

"Wait a minute, Nutty. The guy is discouraged, not disabled. He still has some pride."

"Oh. Pride. Why didn't you say so?" Suddenly Nutty's head popped up, and his shoulders jerked back.

"Wait. No. Now you look like an army officer, for crying out loud. Think about it. He's hurting, but he doesn't want to show it too much. Go back and come in and then speak for him."

Nutty shook his head and then trudged back to the "door." He opened it and came in, let his shoulders sag, and then brought them back up a little.

"Good," William said. "Now speak to me."

Nutty crossed the room rather sadly—maybe tragically—his face full of anguish. In the deepest voice he could make, he said, "Times are real bad . . . honey." He glanced up to see what William thought of that, just as a little smile sneaked across William's face. "Hey, quit laughing. I was just trying to sound like . . ." But now he was smiling himself.

William fought it for a few seconds, tried to speak, but then he dropped his head down on his arms, on the desk, and laughed about as hard as Nutty had ever seen him laugh. When he finally looked up, he said, "'Times are real bad, honey'?" And he started to laugh all over again.

"Well, I don't know. What's he supposed to say? That's what guys say on television. How about, 'I'm sure stuck with an ugly little wife'?"

William was trying to get himself under control. He looked away from Nutty for a while, and then he said, quite seriously, "Well, okay. It's a start. We'll have to keep working on your acting every day. Maybe right now we ought to give your wardrobe some thought. Do you have any dark glasses?"

"I had some but I lost 'em."

"Okay. Maybe we can go buy some. You ought to get started wearing those tomorrow. We can move you into the other stuff gradually, as we get it. You don't want to change all at once."

"What do you mean change, William? I don't want to change."

"Sure you do. That's what this movie star thing is all about. We've got until school starts next fall to get kids thinking differently about you. Right now you couldn't win an election, no matter what you did."

"What good will dark glasses do?"

"It's all part of the image. You're a Hollywood actor now. But there's another element. If everyone decides you've gotten arrogant, the whole thing could backfire on you. What you want is to have people say, 'He's a movie star, but he's still a nice guy. It hasn't gone to his head at all.' And that means you've got to be a nicer person. You've got to treat everyone really well—even Orlando. You can't be heard putting him down, the way you usually do. And try to make up with people like Mindy."

"William, she's hated me for six years. I can't help that."

"Sure you can. Tomorrow you go up to her and you apologize. And make sure other people hear you. Be so nice people will start to think that maybe you've learned your lesson. At first they won't believe it, but gradually you can change their minds."

William had finally asked too much. Nutty would wear shades, if he had to, but he couldn't see himself going around like some little sweetheart. "Hey, no way, William. I'm not going to fake like I'm something I'm not."

"Nutty, you came to me a few days ago and said that the children at the lab school are making fun of you, saying you haven't been a good president. And they're all enamored with this Harpoon fellow."

"Lance."

"Yes, whatever," William said. "But I've offered you a way to beat him at his own game. You're now a movie star. But the other part of it is that you have to be liked. That means treating people with more care than you have in the past."

Nutty thought about that. He knew William had a point. "But, William, I don't even know what I could say to Mindy."

"Well, why don't you try, 'Times are real hard, honey'?"

Nutty punched William for that one. But it didn't matter. William just kept laughing.

Chapter 7

Wiilliam helped Nutty find a pair of sunglasses, and the next morning Nutty wore them to school. He no more than got inside the building, however, before he realized he couldn't see very well in the hallway, and he didn't take three steps before Orlando spotted him. "I don't blame you for trying to hide today," he said. "But those glasses aren't going to do it. Maybe you should try a gorilla costume."

Nutty walked over to Orlando. "Shut up, okay?" he whispered. "I could have squealed on you yesterday, and you'd be in big trouble now."

"No way, man," Orlando said. "I didn't fall through anyone's ceiling."

Nutty took a deep breath. He didn't want to lose his temper. "Orlando, if I'd told who was with me, you guys would have been in almost as much trouble as I am. So don't start giving me a bad time."

"Who me? I never give you a bad time, Nutty. You

know that." Orlando grinned. "Did your parents go nuts?"

"Yeah, they did. And it wasn't funny."

But Orlando seemed to find plenty to laugh about. "I can just hear your dad. I'll bet he gave you a nine-hour speech. 'Freddie, I never thought a son of mine would do anything to embarrass me this way. Listening in on people, crashing through ceilings—it's all very disappointing.'" Orlando knew Mr. Nutsell's style. He sounded a lot like him.

But Nutty was in no mood to hear this kind of stuff, let alone laugh at it. "Orlando, I threw a pair of my gym socks in my locker a couple of months ago. They've gotten some mildew in them, and they really smell bad. Would you please stop by my locker long enough to eat one of them?"

"Hey, you can eat my shorts instead, okay?" Orlando replied.

But just then Nutty saw a couple of girls from his class walk by. Nutty knew he had to be careful. This was just the sort of stuff William had warned him about. He suddenly clamped a hand down on Orlando's shoulder and said, "Hey, buddy, I was only kidding. You're a good friend."

Orlando seemed to take this for sarcasm. He pushed Nutty's hand away and said, "Don't be a jerk, Nutty."

Nutty smiled at the girls and nodded, and then he said to Orlando, rather loudly, "Orlando, I mean it. You're the best friend I've ever had."

Orlando mumbled something about Nutty acting weird, but Nutty was watching the girls—Carrie and

Ami. They seemed to pay no attention to what he had said. "What are the glasses for, Nutty?" Carrie said. "Are you hoping we won't know who you are?"

Nutty was ready to invite Carrie to take a bite out of the same socks. But something inside told him that he really did want people to like him again. He better play it William's way.

"Carrie," Nutty said. "Could I talk to you a sec?"

She stopped and looked at him strangely. She was almost as tall as Nutty, and she leveled her eyes at him, as though she were trying to guess what he was up to.

"Wouldn't you rather just follow us and listen in on our conversation?" Ami said, and she gave Nutty a false little smile.

"No. But I do want to tell you I'm sorry about that. I never should have done it, and now I feel rotten."

Both girls were staring at him, obviously confused, and neither could come up with anything to say for a time.

Orlando started to laugh, however, and the girls took that as their clue that Nutty was acting smart. "Take a hike, Nutty," Carrie said. "You're not sorry one bit."

"Actually, I really am. Honest."

But Carrie was looking at Orlando. "What are you laughing about? From what I've heard, you were in on it. I think you listened to us, too."

Orlando hesitated, and Nutty jumped in. "Don't bring Orlando into this," he said. "I didn't need any help to think up something that dumb."

Carrie and Ami still couldn't find the right response.

They seemed to sense that Nutty was trying to be sincere, but they weren't really buying it. "You may not need help to do something dumb," Ami said, "but you've got plenty of it when you hang around with Orlando."

The girls walked away, as Orlando shouted after them that Nutty had some dirty socks they could eat. But Nutty stopped him. "Let's just lay off that stuff, okay?" he said.

Orlando took a long look at him. "What's going on, Nutty? Are you trying to act like a nice person or something? It won't work. Everybody knows you."

That was probably right. All the same, a few minutes later he got another test of his new "image." When he walked into class, Mrs. Smiley told him that he should put the dark glasses away, that they weren't appropriate in school. Nutty sat down and took them off and then tucked them in his hair on top of his head.

Mindy had twisted in her seat to see him. She rolled her eyes in disgust, and then she said, "Oh, sure. What are you trying to be?"

Nutty hadn't exactly enjoyed the little exchange with Carrie and Ami, but he had no desire at all to bow down to Mindy. He pretended not to hear her and looked away.

"I'll bet you've been crying all night, and you had to cover up your red eyes," Mindy said.

"I'll bet you—" No, he couldn't do this.

"You bet what?"

"Look, Mindy, let's just forget it, okay?"

"Forget what?"

"All this... stuff. I'm sorry I listened to you guys yesterday. I won't do it again."

"You bet you won't. My dad said we could sue you. You're just lucky you didn't land right on one of us and break someone's back or something like that."

Nutty nodded. Finally he forced himself to say, "I know." And actually he had thought about that. He really did regret the whole thing, when he thought of it that way. He just didn't want to have to listen to Mindy.

"I was nervous all night last night. I couldn't even sleep. I just kept thinking about you crashing down like that. If you'd broken any of my bones, my dad would have had you thrown in jail. That's exactly what he said."

"Okay. And I would have deserved it. I already told you I'm sorry."

"Nutty, you're not sorry. You just—"

"Mindy, lay off. He said he was sorry, okay? What more do you want?"

Nutty looked around at Allison. She was usually fairly quiet. He couldn't believe she would take his side that way. He nodded to her, and she sort of smiled. He actually felt pretty good about it—but strange. Very strange.

The rest of the day went a little better. Nutty waited for all the comments he expected from the girls, and every time he simply said he was sorry. The girls didn't exactly accept his apology, but they were at least baffled by the approach. It just wasn't what they expected from any of the guys. At the very least it took the pleasure out of their insults.

Nutty was starting to feel pretty good about the whole thing until Lance walked up to him during lunch and said, "Nutty, I heard you apologize to Mindy. I'm proud of you." But he was smiling, as though he meant something more than he was saying.

Nutty thought of inviting Lance to his locker for a little chew on his socks, but since Nutty had vowed not to get smart with people, he just sort of shrugged and walked away. He was pretty sure the guy was faking the whole thing. How in the world could a guy go around like that—pretending to be nice and everything, pretending to be someone he wasn't?

Nutty had one thing going for him that got him through the day and through the weekend. One of these days the word was going to come out that he was about to appear in a movie, and even if the girls still hated him, they at least would be jealous. That was not so bad. He was getting out of town too. Going to California—beaches, palm trees, sunshine. He couldn't wait to see the movie stars and limousines, all the mansions and fancy restaurants. Every kid in the class was going to die when they realized that they couldn't be in on it. Especially Mindy. What a great thought!

On Saturday Nutty managed to talk his mom into taking him and William into Kansas City. He said he had to have some new clothes for his trip. She was just thrilled that Nutty would buy something besides

T-shirts. But after the shopping, when they met at the appointed time near the doors to the mall and Nutty showed up with his purchases, she was stunned.

He had a couple of shirts that looked as if they were right out of *Gentleman's Quarterly.* They were heavy-looking things, rugged, with natural fibers, of course. "They're all cotton, Freddie," Mrs. Nutsell said. "I'll have to iron them every time you wear them."

"No, not at all," William said. "They're supposed to look wrinkled like that."

But Mrs. Nutsell was too shocked to comment. She had now pulled a pair of shorts from the sack. "Shorts, Freddie? You never wear shorts. You tell me the guys would make fun of you."

"I know. But the man said that's the only thing guys wear in California this time of year."

"Maybe so, but they look expensive, and you'll probably never wear them around Warrensburg."

"I'm going to pay you back with the money I get," Nutty said, avoiding the other issue.

But William said, "He's going to start wearing some new things in town now, Mrs. Nutsell. As a movie actor, he can set the trends. He doesn't have to worry so much what the other boys think of his taste. They'll probably all feel they have to follow him, as a matter of fact."

"William, he's not exactly a 'movie actor' yet," Mrs. Nutsell said. "He's only doing one scene. He may never get another chance."

"Oh, trust me, this is just the beginning, Mrs. Nutsell. Your boy is destined for fame. He'll be a rich young

man in another couple of years and a household name."
William pushed his hands into his pockets and looked
very sure of himself, but then, he always did.

Nutty suddenly thought of the name William was
talking about and thought he better change the subject.
Mom had no idea that he was changing his name for
the movies. "I got some shoes, too."

But Mom had thought of the same thing. "You're not
going to use Nutty for a name, are you? You'll be Freddie Nutsell, won't you? Or maybe Fred?"

"I'll always be Freddie, Mom."

"Actually, though, his stage name is Parker House,"
said William.

"What? Parker House?" Mrs. Nutsell asked.

"Yes, ma'am."

"That's a dinner roll."

"Yes, well, it is kind of catchy in that regard," William
said. "It has a familiarity that will . . ."

"A dinner roll?" Nutty gasped. "William, you didn't
tell me that."

"Oh, didn't I? I guess I thought you knew. But then,
I guess there are lots of rolls and lots of names. There's
Kaiser, for instance, we could have called you that."
He chuckled.

Now William was the one changing the subject. But
Nutty let it go. Everything was so crazy. Why shouldn't
he be named after a dinner roll? Mom said they better
not mention that one to Dad just yet. He had been
talking about the Nutsell name becoming famous.

But when Monday evening came, on the front page
was a picture of Parker House himself. The cap-

tion under the picture read, "Local Boy Begins Movie Career." The business about Parker House showed up later in the story. Dad was so thrilled by all the rest that he only made a mild protest about the name. Nutty told him maybe they would only use that name for his first job. Once he was "established," he could use any name he wanted.

Mr. Nutsell accepted that, and he enjoyed the evening. Every time anyone in the family hung up the phone, it rang again, and most of the calls were to Mom or Dad. All their friends were calling to say how happy and proud they were. Some of Nutty's friends also called, and so did some of Susie's.

Poor Susie had a miserable evening. Just thinking of Nutty going to Hollywood and being on TV was bad enough, but all the extra attention was almost more than she could stand. And that, of course, added an extra little pleasure to the evening for Nutty.

Chapter 8

Nutty wore his new clothes to school the next morning—even the shorts. He had expected some razzing, but it didn't happen. In fact, Nutty was big stuff from the moment he walked through the front doors. A group of girls was standing just inside. Nutty didn't know whether they were actually waiting for him, but they certainly reacted when they saw him.

"Nutty, are you really going to be in a movie?" were the first words he heard.

"Don't call him Nutty," Carrie said. "His name is Parker now." She laughed, and Nutty thought she was teasing, but her tone had changed entirely from what it had been lately.

Nutty came to a stop, and all the girls came toward him. A couple of sixth-grade girls he knew had come in behind him, and they stopped too. And then a whole crowd began to form, kids coming from all directions. He still had his shades on; he wished he had a hood all the way over his head. This was embarrassing. But kind of nice too.

"Parker's just a name we made up," Nutty said. "Don't call me that."

"I like it," Zoie said. "It's better than Nutty."

"Well, I don't know. I've just always been—"

"What's the movie about?" April asked. "What's the name of it?"

Nutty couldn't believe it. April was looking at him as if he were some kind of hero. Two days ago she had been ready to kill him. "I'm not sure what it's about," he said. "It's called *Country Style.* I'm just going to be in this one scene. It's not really such a big deal."

"Are you kidding?"

"Not a big deal?"

Everyone was talking at once, and Nutty just kept looking around, sort of overwhelmed. More people were coming too.

"Nutty," Carrie said, above the others, "how can you say that? You're going to Hollywood. You're a movie star."

"I don't know, Carrie. I'm going to do my best, but—"

"You will, Nutty," someone said, and everyone else was quick to agree.

"Look how he's dressed this morning. He looks so California, I can't believe it."

And then someone, somewhere, in the crowd, said, "He's always been the cutest boy in the school." This brought on a whole lot of laughter, but no one disagreed.

Nutty was liking this more and more.

"How did it happen, Nutty? Who discovered you?" Carrie kept crowding in closer.

Nutty knew he didn't want to explain all that. Nor was he going to mention William. "I don't know. I got an agent—out in California. He found the part for me."

"Really? How did you know how to do that?"

Nutty noticed a few guys hanging around. A couple of sixth graders—Shawn somebody and Jonathan Markley—were looking at him as if they hated him. Nutty knew he better get away from this crowd before some of the guys thought he was being a show-off.

"Well, I guess we better get to class," Nutty said, and he tried to take a step away. But he turned almost directly toward Mindy, who had come up without his noticing her. He expected some sort of slam now, but he figured he could handle it today. Seeing her misery would be worth it.

"Nutty, is it true?" Mindy said. "Are you really going to be in a movie?"

"Yeah." Nutty nodded, trying not to sound cocky. "I'll be going out to California later this week."

"Wow. It's a dream come true," Mindy said.

This was strange. Nutty wasn't sure what she was up to. "I guess so," he said. "Actually, I never thought much about it."

"Really? I always thought you might do something like that."

"Me?"

"Sure. Everyone always says you're cute. You know that."

Nutty wondered whether some of that ceiling did hit her in the head.

"Hey, you're the guy who listens in on us—you ought to know what we say." She was smiling with every tooth she had.

Nutty was really confused now. Was this the insult? Had she been setting him up? "Not usually, Mindy. I feel bad about what I did. I was just—"

"Nutty, don't worry about it. It's pretty funny when you think about it. If you get to be a big star, I'll be able to tell people you drop in on me all the time. That's what my dad told me." This got a big laugh, especially from Mindy herself.

Nutty had lost the power of speech. Girls were all around him, and some were saying he was not Nutty anymore; he was Parker. He decided to move on down the hall. The sky was overcast that morning, and the halls were dark. Nutty could barely see, but he was surrounded by enough "escorts" that he couldn't get lost. They didn't leave even when he stopped at his locker.

It was there that Nutty finally saw Orlando, Richie, and Bilbo. He gave them a weak sort of grin, over the heads of his admirers. "Just a minute," he said. "I'll be right with you." He dug some stuff out of his locker and then walked over to the guys, pulling the mob along with him.

"Ooooooh, a movie star," Orlando said. "Can I have your autograph?"

Nutty had to push a little to get through the crowd and over to Orlando. "Hey, look," he whispered, "I don't want any of this stuff. They just—"

"What the heck's going on?" Orlando asked. "Why didn't you tell us about this movie thing?"

"It just happened. I didn't know until a couple of days ago."

But that wasn't quite good enough. Orlando was looking disgusted—or disappointed. "Who dressed you?" he said.

"This is just...you know."

"No. I don't know. You'll have to tell me how things are for Hollywood stars."

"Hey, come on, Orlando." But Orlando was walking away. Bilbo and Richie had gone ahead of him.

"Nutty," one of the girls was saying, "are there any big stars in the movie you're making?"

Nutty mumbled that he didn't know, and then he headed for the classroom, where he knew Mrs. Smiley would stop all this. But the surprise of the morning was still waiting. When Nutty got to class, his shades still on, Mrs. Smiley didn't say one thing about getting rid of them. She walked over to his desk immediately. "Nutty, I'm so excited for you," she said.

Nutty gave a little smile and a nod.

"Listen, before class starts, I want to ask you a favor. I have three nieces in Kansas City who just aren't going to believe that one of my own students is a movie actor. Would you mind too much signing an autograph for them—and one for my daughter?"

Nutty took the first slip of paper Mrs. Smiley offered and was about to sign when she said, "Oh, don't write 'Nutty,' okay? They'll be hearing about you as Parker

House. Why don't you write that? And could you write a little message to each. The first one is named Renee."

Nutty stared at the paper for a time, and finally he wrote, "Lots of luck to Renee, Parker House." He looked up, as if to say, "Is that all right?" Mrs. Smiley looked entirely satisfied. She handed him another slip of paper.

Just then Nutty glanced over and saw Sarah sliding into her seat. She smiled, and then, when Nutty sort of shrugged, she laughed. Nutty thought maybe she understood. This really wasn't his idea.

The most welcome thing Nutty heard all morning was the bell ringing. Mrs. Smiley, as usual, got down to business. Nutty was glad to have a little time to think. He had expected a little attention that morning, but nothing like this. He liked it—a little—but he also hated it. A lot. He thought of throwing the whole thing over, just so his friends wouldn't hate him—and Mindy would.

School was a waste that day. Nutty couldn't concentrate at all. During recess he tried to talk to Orlando and the guys to tell them he wasn't trying to go "Hollywood" on them. But there were two problems with that. First, he was wearing what the guys considered some very strange clothes in light of the fact that Nutty had never worn anything but jeans and T-shirts his whole life. And, second, he was being mobbed again, mostly by girls but even by guys who wanted to know how he had pulled this off.

It was only after school that Nutty managed to get away from everyone and then head over to Orlando's house. He found Bilbo hanging out there too, and Lance! All day Nutty had sort of watched Lance. He had stayed away from everything, and he hadn't said much. Nutty couldn't tell whether he was jealous or mad or uninterested in the whole thing or what.

But now Lance said, "Hey, Nutty, congratulations." He actually stuck out his hand for a handshake.

Nutty shook his hand and said, "Thanks."

"How did you get the part?" Lance asked.

The guys were in Orlando's backyard, sitting on the patio in lawn chairs. Nutty glanced at Bilbo, who was stretched out on a chaise lounge, grinning. "I don't know. I just contacted a man in California."

"Where did you get the idea to do that?" Lance asked.

Why did this guy always sound so nice? "Well, I just . . . thought of it."

"Wait a minute," Orlando said. He stood up. "Now I know. I've been trying to think what the heck is going on. But it's William, isn't it? He thought this up for you."

"What makes you think that?"

"Nutty, you'd never in a million years think of writing to some guy in California about being in a movie. But William would. I just don't get what you're trying to do."

"He's trying to start a great career, I'd say," Lance said. "I think he's playing it smart."

"Yeah, well, you've got to be smart to play it smart."

"Hey, Orlando, Nutty's going to be rich before long. Then you'll know who's smart," Lance said, looking back at Nutty. "You'll love southern Cal. I used to live out there. I envy you."

Nutty sort of nodded, and then Lance said he had to leave. He patted Nutty on the shoulder, congratulated him one more time, and said good-bye. Nutty waited until he had gone through the gate, and then he said, "Can you believe that guy? I never met anybody that phony."

"He's not a bad guy," Bilbo said.

"I think he's a great guy," Orlando added, and seemed to mean "compared to some guys I know."

"What's all that handshaking stuff, and 'You'll love southern Cal'?" Nutty asked, trying to imitate the smoothness of Lance's style.

Orlando cracked up. "Oh, right. Right. You're standing there in a wimpy pair of shorts, a Mr. Hollywood shirt—plus shades—and you're talking about being a phony?"

"Yeah. Where did you get those clothes?" Bilbo asked.

Nutty suddenly hated the stuff he had on. "Well, you know. They want you to . . . look a certain way."

"Who, Nutty?" Orlando asked. "Tell us who wants you to look that way. Because I think it's William."

"Well, yeah, partly. And then—"

"I knew it. This whole thing is another one of William's plans. What's it for, Nutty? What do you want?"

Bilbo answered. "To be a movie star, obviously."

"Yeah, but I know Nutty. He wants something else. I think this all has to do with Lance. I think Nutty couldn't stand to see Lance come in and take over as the big shot."

"No way," Nutty argued. "It was just something—"

But he decided to let it drop. Orlando could think whatever he wanted to think, especially when he was right.

Chapter 9

Nutty was looking out the window. He had flown on airplanes a couple of times before, but he still found it exciting. Below him were the Rocky Mountains, which reminded him of his big ski trip a few months back.

But William brought him back to reality. "Nutty, I think we better try these lines again."

Suddenly Nutty felt sick—and not airsick. All week he and William had been working on Nutty's acting, but he wasn't making much progress. The lines for the actual scene in the film were being rewritten, so Nutty didn't have those. But the woman who called said not to worry about that. "It's not a big part. We'll run through it a few times, and you'll have it."

But she kept referring to him as an "actor," and Nutty knew better. William had tried to imagine a possible scene, and he had written his own little production that he and Nutty had been working on.

"All right," William said. "Shut your eyes. Let's try this again. I think you're getting closer."

Nutty shut his eyes all right, but he wasn't buying the encouragement. William was just trying to build up his confidence.

"Okay. Picture the living room in the old farmhouse," William said. "Try to zero in on the way it looks: the old couch with a blanket thrown over it; on the wall, the picture of a red barn and a little pond; the flowered wallpaper. Get the smell of baking bread in your mind."

Nutty wondered about that. They bought theirs at Safeway.

What he was really smelling was the rubbery chicken that had been served for lunch. He was tasting it too—for the second time.

"Okay. You've done the morning chores," William said. "It's a hot summer day. You've come in to rest for just a few minutes. You know you have a long day ahead, with lots of work to do out in the hot sun. You and your father have come to a time of crisis. He wants you to take over the farm someday, but you want to be a rock star. Your father hates everything about rock music; he gets furious when he hears you practicing your guitar at night. But for you, music is your life."

"Geez, William. Music is my life?" Nutty said.

"Feel it, Nutty. Feel that need to get away from all this."

"That I can feel."

"Hate those fields, that burning sun. Hate everything about your life. But don't hate your father. I want you

79

to feel a terrific sense of ambiguity toward the man. I want you to love him, and I want you to hate him." William paused, dramatically. "All right. He just came through the door. Keep your eyes shut, and I'll read his lines. I'm going to give you about thirty seconds first. Get yourself all the way into those emotions, and then I'll come in."

Oh, sure, Nutty thought. I hate my dad; I love my dad. And I'm thirty thousand feet in the air, swallowing down boomerang chicken.

"Warren, what are you doing in here? We have work to do," William said.

"I know, Pa. I'll be right there." Nutty still had his eyes shut. He was waiting for William's next line, but it didn't come. Nutty finally opened his eyes and looked over at him.

"Nutty, you sound like you memorized that."

"That's because I did."

"But try to sound like you didn't."

"I think it's too late. If you wanted me to do that, you shouldn't have made me memorize it."

"No, no, no. You have to memorize your lines, but an actor has to make them sound real."

"Yeah, but I'm not an actor."

"You are, starting tomorrow."

Nutty shook his head. They had been over all this twenty times this week. "Look, William, I'm doing the best I can." He turned and looked out the window.

William was obviously not pleased. He sat quietly for some time, and then he finally said, "Listen, Nutty, maybe it's hard to do here on the airplane, but to-night—at the hotel—we've got to do a lot of work. If we have to stay up all night, we're going to have to get you past this block you seem to have."

"William, what are you talking about?" Nutty said.

"We're going to be in Hollywood. I want to have a look around. I want to see those stars in the sidewalks and that Chinese restaurant, or whatever it is, where movie stars stick their feet in the cement."

"I'm going to stick both your feet in cement and let it set, if you don't start taking all this seriously."

But that's where William was wrong. Nutty was serious—completely. He just couldn't do it. And by tomorrow he was going to be in more than cement—up to his chin—without any help from William. But he didn't think more practice was going to help. That only seemed to make him nervous.

"Probably, once you get on the set with the other actors, and get some help from a good director, you'll be okay. I just think we need to do all we can before then."

Nutty didn't argue. He really didn't know what would help.

"Now remember, too, there's a certain style to all this. You have to seem like a movie star. Kiss everyone you meet, but don't really. Just sort of kiss the air next to people's cheeks and say, 'So nice to meet you.' And show a little style. I know your hair looks a little strange, and you're supposed to be the red-blooded-boy type, but they expect you to have some presence."

"Presents?"

"Not presents. Presence. A sense that you are somebody. Watch what everyone else does. You'll get the feel of things."

Nutty felt sick to his stomach. If William had made him cut his hair up high above the ears and dye it brown and then put on this stupid jacket, filled with padding—all for nothing—he was going to stick the guy under cement.

But everything seemed much more promising once Nutty and William were climbing into the big, black limousine. True, the driver had fussed a little. "They told me I was picking up a kid and a grown man. You ain't no grown man." But William had assured him that he was William Bilks, and the driver shrugged and got in the car. Now they were flying down the freeway with thousands of other cars, and outside Nutty could see palm trees and sunshine. It was just the way he had expected. True, inland, he could see a rusty-colored haze over everything, but smog in Los Angeles was something he had heard about. He wasn't going to worry about that.

"How long will it take us to get to Hollywood?" Nutty asked the driver.

"Hollywood?" the driver said. "You ain't going to Hollywood. You're going to Burbank."

"How come?"

"Hey, I just drive this thing. They told me to take you to a hotel up in Burbank."

"I'm sure that's closer to the studio," William said. "Lots of studios are in Burbank. It's not far from Hollywood."

"That's right," the driver said. "Hollywood's just a few miles over. You don't want to go over there anyway. Hollywood's nothing."

"Nothing?" Nutty said. "What do you mean?"

"Just what I said. Beverly Hills and over that way—that's nice. But Hollywood's just a run-down old town."

"What about the stars in the sidewalk and all that?" Nutty asked.

"They're just stars made out of brass or something, stuck in the sidewalk. It ain't much to see."

"But we're going to go over there, aren't we? I want to see some movie stars."

"What would they be doing in Hollywood?"

Nutty sat back and looked out the window. He wasn't going to talk to this guy anymore. He had a bad attitude; that was all. But the drive didn't seem quite so exciting now. The traffic had bogged down to a crawl, and all Nutty knew now was that he was heading for some place called Burbank.

As it turned out, the driver's attitude hadn't been negative enough. Nutty hadn't been able to calm his excitement completely until he got stuck in a hotel room in Burbank all evening—with William. The two of them did go out for a walk, but there wasn't much to see. Nutty wanted to take a taxi to Hollywood, but William said they didn't have time. They needed to practice.

So all evening Nutty practiced "I know, Pa" and the rest of his lines. William had written a big crisis scene in which Warren, farm-boy-turned-rock-musician, announced that he was leaving the farm to go off to follow his dream. The father was supposed to yell for a while and then start to cry, and then Warren was supposed to break down and cry too. But William was, if anything, a worse actor than Nutty. He was so funny when he tried to get emotional that Nutty would lose his concentration. And then William would get mad. And then the whole process would start over again.

William finally lost his temper completely. He told Nutty he was on his own, and Nutty said that was fine and turned on the television set. But TV showed the same stuff in California that it did in Missouri. Dull stuff. And when the woman from the studio called and said that Nutty would be picked up at five in the morning so he could go to wardrobe and get made up for an eight o'clock start, William told Nutty he better turn off the TV and get a good night's sleep.

"Hot night in California!" Nutty muttered as he prepared for bed. But as he lay in bed, he told himself he might as well not get uptight. He would just relax and give it his best shot. He was going to have as much fun as he could and then forget all about this whole movie career thing. If they filmed at eight, maybe by ten or so he could talk someone into taking him over to Hollywood, and he and William could look around. Things were bound to turn out all right.

That's what he told himself. "Things can't get any worse," he kept saying. But they could. And they did.

The limousine showed up on time. That was the only thing that went right the next morning. When he got to the makeup room and a woman started slapping gooey stuff all over his face and making up his eyes, he was not pleased. But when another woman brought in a red plaid shirt, overalls, and an old straw hat, he started to panic. He never should have asked, "Where

84

are my shoes?" because the answer was "You don't wear any."

"Hey, I thought I was a farm kid, not some kind of hillbilly."

"Look, kid, I just work here. Don't throw one of your child-star tantrums on me. I've taken enough of that stuff to last me forever."

She was a big woman with a voice like a rumbling cannon. Nutty wasn't about to say anything else to her. He sort of gulped and looked over at William. When the woman walked away for a minute, he said, "William, I guess you're going to tell me that she's one of the people I'm supposed to kiss?"

"Of course not." William was still mad from the night before.

"William, look at me. I'm dressed up like I'm going to be on 'Hee-Haw.'"

"Hush, Nutty. They'll hear you."

But Nutty didn't care. He was getting mad.

A young woman showed up shortly after that and led him out to the set. It was something out of a bad high-school play: an old red barn with a rickety fence and a stack of hay. Didn't they know about bales out here in California? Who stacked hay anymore?

People were moving around, getting set up. Guys were moving booms around, changing the lights. For a moment Nutty did feel a little excitement. And then a skinny little guy walked onto the set and said, "Where's the kid who's playing the hayseed?"

"William," Nutty whispered, "let's try your lines again. I think I can cry now."

85

Chapter 10

Nutty was about to find out what the word *chaos* meant. An intense, nervous man with buggy little eyes gave him a script and told him to get his lines ready. The man made it sound as though shooting would start in a matter of minutes. Nutty and William walked well away from the set and read through the lines a couple of times. As it turned out, Nutty had only six lines, and they were much simpler than the stuff William had written. Emotion was the least of his concerns, since the whole point of the dialogue was merely to give some "city slicker" directions.

"This is stupid," Nutty said. "Nobody talks like this."

"I know," William said. "It's the worst kind of stereotyping. It's demeaning to farmers and Midwesterners in general. When I get the chance, I'll have a talk with the director. I can't believe he'll allow this sort of thing."

Nutty had bigger worries. He was trying to imagine what people back home would think of him once they saw the part he was playing. Movie star? In overalls and a straw hat? And every line starting with "Ah, shucks"?

"Let's run through these lines a couple more times, Nutty. But let's drop all the 'shucks' and 'derns' and 'yups' and 'nopes,' and try to give it more of a contemporary sound."

"A what?"

"You know. Try to talk more like a normal kid."

William took a pen from his pocket and started slashing and editing. Then he and Nutty tried the lines several more times. Once Nutty could remember them pretty well, William stopped him. "Let's get back to the set so we're ready when they are," he said. "It's better if you don't get this entirely memorized this time. Just listen to the director and learn from him. But try to make this part into something a little better than it appears on the surface. I think you can give it some depth if you think of the boy as someone like Warren— a boy who longs for a better life."

Right now that was something Nutty could understand.

So the boys returned to the set and got ready. Two hours later they were still waiting. They had found a couple of old wooden chairs on another set, and they had watched as people had shouted and yelled at each other, the lighting had been adjusted, problems with the sound system had been corrected, the whole set had been rearranged, and the actor who was going to be the "city slicker" had thrown a tantrum.

Through it all the director had acted approximately

the way monkeys behave in cages at the zoo. He ran around, screeched, waved his arms—did everything but swung through the rafters by his tail. He used language Nutty had only heard when he walked by the high school, and he called everyone in sight names that should have gotten him poked in the nose. He had drunk enough coffee to fill a bathtub, except that he had spilled half of it, and he had run to the telephone at least twenty times.

A couple of times Nutty had gotten up to take a little walk, just to get off the old chair, and both times, the man had screamed: "Don't you go wandering off now. When I get ready to shoot, I'm not going to go looking for you." And then for no reason at all, he had called Nutty "a spoiled-brat actor type."

But, finally, when Nutty was starting to wonder whether it wasn't time for lunch, the director had demanded that he come onto the set immediately.

"All right now," he said, pacing and thinking. "Tell me your name." He was little, but he had a powerful stare that seemed to reach out at Nutty.

"Nut . . . or, I mean, Parker House."

"Parker House? Who made that up?"

"Uh . . . an agent guy."

"It doesn't matter. I don't think you're right for this. You sound like you're from LA. Where are you from anyway?"

"Missouri."

"Well, then, talk like it. I want to hear a whole lot more nasal in your voice. And I want you to mumble your words—drawl them out long and slow. You've been looking at me all bright-eyed and lively. What I need is half-open eyes, a dumb stare. Tuck your thumbs in your overalls and give me a don't-know-nothing kind of look. Have you got that?"

Nutty nodded, tucked his thumbs in the straps of his overalls and tried to look stupid.

"No, no. Don't exaggerate," the director said, throwing his clipboard on the floor and cursing. "Why can't I ever get what I need around here? Who does the casting? Just once, I'd like to get an actor to work with." He threw his head back and stared at the ceiling—just stood there in utter silence. But his eyes and his bushy mustache were twitching around as if he were about to have a nervous breakdown. Nutty thought seriously of telling him to drop dead, but he didn't do it. He just waited.

"Okay, okay," the director said. "Let's get you over here by this haystack."

When Nutty walked closer, he could see the stuff was really straw, not hay, but he supposed it didn't make much difference. Nothing else made any sense.

"I'm not bringing Harry out here until you're ready. The guy will give me nothing but garbage if you're not up to speed."

Nutty nodded. He thought Harry must be the other actor, but he wasn't even sure.

"I'm going to have this young lady read Harry's lines, and I want you to give me a feel for how you read yours. But let's have the right look this time."

Nutty tried to look dumb but not quite as dumb as he looked last time.

"Well, all right. Let your mouth fall a little slack, but don't hang your jaw onto your chest. Yes. There it is. All right, son. I can live with that. Yes. Hold that." He walked closer. "What was your name again?"

"Parker House."

"Right. Park, my boy, I've grown fond of you. I'm getting some very nice vibrations here. I think you and I can work together. I want to shoot this scene without a lot of grief on anyone's part. You can call me Damian, all right?"

Nutty had a couple of other names in mind.

"I can see that you're willing to listen and learn," the director said. "I like that. So listen to me now." He was whispering, but he was gesturing vigorously with his hands. "Here's what I want. Think of yourself as something more than a stone, something less than a dumb animal. I want semiconsciousness. I want an IQ flirting with the negative. This is crucial, Park. We're not playing this for slaps on the knee. What we want is a turning point. Harry finds in you a symbol of his frustrations in coming from the city into this culturally deprived, ignorant country existence. He must see in you a wasteland; his disillusionment must crystalize in this single moment. Can you feel that, Park? Do you have an inkling of what I'm trying to do here?"

"Uh . . . yeah, I think so."

"Don't play the part yet, Park. Talk to me. Tell me how you see this, what you're feeling."

"I guess I'm supposed to act sort of dumb."

The director suddenly spun around and shouted a long stream of profanity. "Why?" he screamed to the ceiling. "Why? Why can't I just once find an actor who comprehends what I'm trying to do? Where's the actor in this world who has some art in him? These people learn to read lines, but they have no soul; I swear they have no soul."

But the man suddenly spun around again. "All right. All right. Park, I'm sorry. I get very frustrated, but I'm here to teach you. You're young. I have to remember that. Let's just try the lines. I think maybe you have a feel for what I'm trying to say to you. You simply can't articulate it. I never met an actor who could say anything that wasn't written for him. Not a single one. All right, Denise, give him the lines."

The young woman, dressed like a gypsy it seemed to Nutty, said she had changed her name to Velvet, but the director paid no attention. She went ahead and read the line.

Nutty gave his, just the way he and William had practiced.

"What? What did you say?" The director was spinning around, trying to find his clipboard. "I rewrote that scene. I know those lines. That's not what I wrote."

"Uh... we changed the 'nope,' and took out the 'shucks.'"

"What are you talking about? You can't do that. Who's we? Who cut those words?"

William had finally heard enough. He came striding onto the set, looking odd as he took such long steps with such little legs and seeming quite out of place in his little gray sweater. "Sir, I worked with Nutty on this. We took—"

91

"Nutty? Who's Nutty? What's Nutty?"

"Excuse me. I mean Parker," William said. "We're both from the Midwest. We've been around farmers. They don't say 'shucks' and 'nope' all the time. They're nothing at all like this. We were just trying to give the part a more contemporary feel, some verisimilitude."

The director suddenly jumped straight in the air and came down screaming. Some of the words weren't clear, but the idea was that he needed air, that he was going to have a stroke if someone didn't bring his blood pressure medicine immediately, and that William should get out of his sight forever. And when he finally started to slow into a language that was a little easier to follow, he said, "Who are you, anyway? Who let you in here?"

"I'm Parker's manager and agent, sir. I arranged to travel with him from Missouri."

"Well, I just unarranged it. You get out of here. You will not ever touch a word of mine again. Give this boy that script. He will follow it word for word. What do you know about art? What are you anyway, some sort of aberration? You talk like my uncle Max, and you look like my sister's third son."

"I'm afraid I'm actually no relative of yours," William said. "At least I have that to be thankful for."

That was that. The director went crazy, kicked William out, fumed and fussed for ten minutes, and then said he had to go rest and have lunch before "my arteries blow up."

So Nutty was ushered off to a little cafeteria, and the director was gone for an hour and a half. When the scene was finally shot, Nutty did it with all the "nopes" and "shuckses," and with his mouth hanging half open and his eyes half shut.

The director called him several dirty names, demanded seventeen retakes, and when all was finished, grabbed Nutty in his arms, hugged him, kissed him on the cheek, and said that Parker was brilliant. "You have a wonderful future," he said. "You have a great feel for this. I hope I didn't scare you or discourage you. I demand the most from an actor. It's why I'm as great as I am. But I'll make you great too. When I find talent, I work with it, bring it along, make it part of me and what I am. Do you want to come along with me to the top?"

Nutty shrugged, which didn't go over all that well, and then he walked back to the makeup room, where a skinny woman with freckles rubbed cream all over his face and then wiped away all the gunk. Nutty had no idea where he was going to find William.

But Nutty had only just gotten up from his chair when something good finally happened; he spotted an actress he actually recognized. He didn't know who she was or where he had seen her—TV, he thought—but he knew he knew her from somewhere. This was his chance. He walked over to her, even though she was just getting dabbed with cream herself.

"Excuse me," Nutty said. "I was wondering if I could get your autograph?" Nutty was thinking that he could salvage something if he could show an autograph of a real TV star when he got back home.

"Are you kidding?" the woman said.

Nutty had begun to doubt himself, but he persisted. "No, not at all."

"Well, all right. Have you got something to write on?"

"Oh. Let's see." Nutty started feeling through his pockets, but he was still in his overalls.

The makeup woman found a slip of paper somewhere and handed it to the actress, who wrote something. On the way to wardrobe Nutty kept trying to read the name, but he couldn't make sense of her scribble. He decided he'd have to work on it later. At least he had something.

Once Nutty was in his street clothes—his shorts and "with it" shirt—he was directed outside to a waiting limousine. A driver was standing by the car. "All right, let's go," he said.

"Where's William?"

"Is that the kid who looks ten and talks fifty?"

"Yeah."

"He's in the car."

Nutty hadn't seen William because of the darkened windows, but he was glad to be back in touch. He opened the door and found William leaning back, his arms folded across his chest.

"Hurry up, Nutty," he said. "We've got to make a flight."

"Flight? Aren't we staying over another night?"

"No. The producer just told me that they aren't paying for the night since your part is finished. We're flying back now."

"It's going to be awful late when we get in. And my parents thought we would—"

94

"I called your parents. They'll be at the airport."

So that was that. Back to the hotel long enough to pick up luggage, a scenic tour of Burbank along the way, the same freeway, and not so much as a glimpse at the letters that spelled out HOLLYWOOD on the side of a hill somewhere out there.

Nutty and William hardly spoke. They were both too upset. "We didn't see a thing," Nutty mumbled after a time.

"Frankly, I'm disillusioned," William said.

"I was hoping we'd at least see some movie stars." But suddenly he remembered the autograph. "Oh, I did get this." He handed the scrap of paper to William and asked whether he could read the name.

"It looks like Allison or Angie or something of that sort. The last name is Boyd."

"Oh, yeah," the driver said, "Allison Boyd. I picked her up at the airport day before yesterday."

"Isn't she on TV?" Nutty asked. "I've seen her before."

"Yeah, she is. She told me she makes commercials. She was shooting some kind of dog food ad this time."

Nutty slumped down in his seat. Now he remembered. He had seen her in a kitchen, down on her hands and knees pleading with a dog to come and eat. But the dog wouldn't eat until she tried Alpo or Kal-Kan or Puppy Chow or one of those.

"Dog food," Nutty said in disgust.

"Yes, exactly," William said.

Chapter 11

William didn't have much to say during the flight home. Nutty went to sleep soon after takeoff. It had been a very long day. But when the stewardess brought dinner, Nutty decided he would have some—even if it didn't look very appetizing.

"Nutty, I've been thinking about this whole matter," William said.

"What whole matter?"

"This entire fiasco we've just been through," William said.

Nutty wondered if they had been through a storm or something; he had no idea what a "fee-ask-o" was.

"We weren't treated well, and I'm afraid your part in the movie is going to be rather embarrassing," William continued. "As it turns out, it's too bad that the thing is going to be on TV so soon."

"Man, I'm going to get laughed out of town."

"Well, now, that's just the point. We've got to find a way to minimize the damage."

THE MOVIE STAR

"I think the damage is done, William."

"In one sense, yes. But we have to keep the whole thing in perspective. You can't help it that the part was weak. An actor has to get started somehow."

"This actor just quit."

"No, no. That would be the worst thing you could do. You have to make light of this silly part and create the idea that it was only a stepping-stone to much more important roles. If you stop now, you won't have any way of saving face."

"No way, William. Parker House is finished with roles. I'm going to take the razzing, and then I'm going to try to forget the whole thing." Nutty was taking a long look at his lasagna. He wondered if the green color was caused by spices or by age. It reminded him of the food at the lab school.

"You'll never be reelected next fall."

"Yeah, well, that doesn't matter so much."

"Lance will be the new president."

Nutty thought about that. "I don't care that much. When all those kids were hanging around me, I didn't like it. I just want to be a regular guy again."

"Well, fine. It really doesn't matter to me. I have more important matters to concern myself with. But as I recall, you came to me a couple of weeks ago, desperate because all the girls were laughing at you and deeply concerned that some new fellow was going to be more popular than you. I believe there was even a certain concern about a particular girl and her attraction to the same fellow."

All the while, William was opening a little packet of salad dressing and squeezing the contents on his salad.

97

He really did sound as though he didn't care either way, but Nutty knew better. William hated being beaten—at anything.

"How did you feel when you found out the girls all thought you were some sort of joke?" William asked.

"Lousy."

"Well, which was worse: being a joke—and a jerk— or being the center of attention?"

"Both were pretty bad."

"Which was worse, Nutty? Tell the truth."

"Being a jerk, of course, but—"

"Okay. Remember that. And here's how to play it. Tell everyone what a fantastic time you had in Hollywood. Say the part you played was really stupid. Prepare them for the worst. But tell them you enjoyed the trip so much that you are hoping to go after better parts. Imply that you already have some things in the works—the possibility of some starring roles."

"Lie, huh?"

"No, not at all. I'm going to keep trying to get you better material."

"It's still a lie."

"It's politics, Nutty. You can't tell them what really happened. You'd never live it down. Part of politics is making your past look as good as you possibly can."

"Tell lies."

William didn't like that. Nutty could tell. William ate his dinner and then sat back and read a book he had brought along, but he didn't say much of anything. The book was called *The Philosophical Foundations of American Politics*. Nutty thought maybe he would read it when William was finished. It was just the thing for a guy who was retiring from the office of Student Council president of his elementary school.

Nutty really didn't want to go to school the next morning. It was Friday, and he had told everyone he wouldn't be back until Monday. But Dad said there was no reason to stay home, and Nutty couldn't tell him that he actually did have a few reasons. The trouble was, they were all reasons Dad wouldn't understand.

So Nutty showed up in time to enter Mrs. Smiley's class just as the bell was ringing. He thought that would take care of everything. But he hadn't counted on Mrs. Smiley's being quite so excited to "hear all about it." She asked him to stand up and tell everyone about Hollywood and what it was like to be in a movie.

Nutty stood up slowly. He was trying hard to think of what he could say. "Well, it's a lot like you'd expect. It's real pretty out there. Palm trees and stuff."

"I guess you were awfully busy with the filming."

"Yeah. We were over there at the studio most of the time. It was just one scene, but it took a long time."

"Well, tell us about it. Was it exciting?"

"Well, I don't know.... It took a lot longer than I expected to get everything set up, and then the director screamed a lot, and everyone was mad about half the time."

"Oh, yes, that's what I've heard. Directors are like that, I guess ... so wild and intense. I think that's how artists tend to be." Mrs. Smiley really wasn't getting the picture. "Maybe it takes that kind of commitment and emotion to bring out the most in actors."

"Yeah, maybe. But really, my part was pretty stupid. I kind of hate to have everyone see it."

"No, no. Don't say that, Nutty. You got your break. You got your foot in the door. This time it was one scene; next time it might be a supporting role. But I've got a feeling your day is coming, and we're all going to say we knew you way back when you were just a kid from Warrensburg."

Nutty could see all the girls making those same kind of eyes that Mrs. Smiley was making—all dreamy and full of visions. Mindy had twisted all the way around in her seat and was looking at Nutty as if he were a giant hot-fudge sundae and she were starving to death. It was scary. Even Richie and Bilbo looked impressed or . . . something, maybe just jealous.

On the other hand, Orlando was doing little gag noises.

"I just hope you won't be disappointed. They had me play this hick sort of kid. That's why my hair is like this."

"I like it that way," Mindy said, but some of the other girls said they liked him better when he was blond.

"Did you meet any movie stars?" Carrie asked. "Did you get any autographs?"

"Uh . . . no."

"Which? You didn't meet any, or you didn't get autographs?" Mrs. Smiley asked. "I guess it isn't the thing to do for one movie actor to ask another for an autograph."

"Yeah, that's right."

"But you did meet some?"

Nutty hesitated. Then he decided to tell the truth, but his lips didn't get the message in time. "Yeah. A couple."

"Who? Who?" The shouts were coming from everywhere, and Mrs. Smiley was telling everyone to quiet down.

"Well, no one too famous."

"But who?"

"Well, that one guy all the girls like. Uh...I can't think of his name. That kid on TV. Cameron or something like that."

Half the girls in the class crashed. Heads dropped onto desks, hands flew to faces, shrieks and moans filled the air. "Kirk Cameron?" Mrs. Smiley asked. "You saw Kirk Cameron? My daughter will just die when she hears that."

"It was no big deal. He just said hi and stuff like that. I didn't talk to him very much."

More crashes, more pain and anguish.

"What's he really like?" Mindy pleaded to know.

"Well, he was pretty nice, you know. He's just sort of a regular guy—once you get to know him."

"No he's not, Nutty," Mindy moaned. "He's an angel."

But others were repeating, "Once you get to know him. . . . Nutty knows Kirk Cameron."

"Well, not that much. I just—"

"Who else? Who else did you see?"

"Oh. Uh...Just...Eddie Murphy."

Nutty saw Richie's head pop around. "Really?" he said.

But Orlando wasn't buying it. "No way. Nutty, you didn't really see him. Where was he?"

"Oh...well, we stayed at the same hotel. He was eating breakfast. I just saw him from a distance. I didn't get acquainted or anything."

"What hotel was it, Nutty?" Mrs. Smiley asked.

"Oh, it was...I can't think of the name of it. It was that pink one you always see in movies."

"The Beverly Hills Hotel?" Mrs. Smiley asked, sounding almost like one of the girls.

"Yeah." Nutty nodded a couple of times. "It's real nice."

"Nice?" she asked.

"Well, yeah. It's fancy. And pink. And everything."

Nutty glanced around. Everybody was staring at him, as if he were an alien visitor or something. The envy was as thick as the makeup he had worn in Hollywood—or Burbank. Except...Orlando looked doubtful, and Lance was hard to read. He was smiling just a little, and he looked a whole lot calmer than anyone else.

Nutty knew he had better shut up right now, before he got in any deeper.

Nutty had avoided looking at Sarah through all this; now he glanced over at her. But she wasn't looking back. She was looking ahead, showing no emotion at all, no reaction. He had a feeling that without looking, she was seeing right through him. Why had he ever started all this?

"Well, Nutty," Mrs. Smiley said, "—or do you want to be called Parker now?"

"Oh, no. Nutty is fine. I'm just the same old guy." But he had just done something sort of weird. He realized he had flipped his head back with a little flair... or something. He had never done anything like that before.

"Well, I'm impressed. This whole thing hasn't gone to your head at all. Aren't you all impressed, class?"

Some of the kids were nodding; others were looking up longingly. Richie was wondering; Bilbo was rolling his eyes; Orlando was sticking his finger down his throat; Lance was smiling that little smile; and Sarah still wouldn't look at him. Nutty didn't know what he thought. He had a feeling Orlando's reaction was the most fitting, but he sort of liked watching Mindy break her little heart too.

Chapter 12

As the next couple of weeks slipped by and Nutty knew the movie would soon be appearing on TV, he made more and more of a point that the part he had played had been small and silly. The truth was, he never wanted another acting job as long as he lived, but it was hard not to enjoy having so many fans—or whatever they were. He had told William he didn't want to lie, but he kept hinting that a television series was in the works for him, along with some major parts in upcoming movies.

Actually, there was one other thing he found himself doing, even though he kept promising himself he wouldn't. He wasn't sure how it kept happening, but the way he regarded his California experience was steadily improving. It was like a fish that grows bigger once it has slithered off the hook and back into deep water. He now had himself half convinced that he actually had had a great time. The extravagant room-service dinners, the relaxing hours by the pool (which somehow grew into an afternoon on the beach), the conversations with movie stars—all of it—started with hints, grew into mentions, and then developed into full-blown stories.

Mindy was buying it all. And so were most of his fans. Sarah wasn't saying much, however, and Nutty didn't know what she was thinking. Lance had somehow slipped into the background, but he seemed quite patient with that. He didn't talk as much as he had at first. When girls crowded around Nutty and listened to his stories, Nutty would spot Lance, smiling, watching. In fact, Nutty got the uneasy feeling that he was waiting for something.

Bilbo and Richie were a little more skeptical. They pointed out a couple of times that Nutty's stories were inconsistent. Hadn't Nutty said at first that Kirk Cameron only said hi? Why didn't he mention such a long conversation at the beginning? But they didn't push the matter too hard. Orlando took care of that for them.

Orlando was disgusted with Nutty's new image from the beginning, but all Nutty's stories practically drove him crazy. One day at lunch the boys were sitting out behind the school, on the lawn. Lance was with them. Orlando started questioning Nutty, really just teasing, but finally he said, "So what's the deal, Nutty? Once you're an actor, are you allowed to make up your life as you go along?"

"What are you talking about?"

Orlando had finished his lunch and was stretched

out on his side, with one hand propping up his head. "Well, you know—if you act when you're making a movie, maybe it's easy to get sort of mixed up and start acting all the time. Maybe you figure if you don't like what's happening in the real world, you can just change the script a little—the way you do in a movie."

"So what are you trying to say, Orlando?"

"I'm just saying that if you keep talking about the great time you had in California, that one-day trip could take two weeks to tell about. I never heard of a guy doing so much in twenty-four hours in my whole life." He was grinning in that annoying way of his. "Nutty, excuse me, but hasn't your nose been growing a little longer lately?"

"Listen, Orlando, don't give me any of that. You're the guy whose batting average always gets better after the season is over."

Orlando sat up. "What? What you are you talking about? You're just jealous because I bat four-fifty. I don't have to—"

"Four-fifty? Orlando, how can you tell me I'm changing my story and then make up something like that? Cut that four-fifty in half, and then start whittling it down to something close to the truth." Nutty turned to Bilbo. "Did Orlando ever hit anywhere near four-fifty?"

"Yeah, I think so, if you add all three of his seasons together," Bilbo said. "That's one-fifty each year."

"No way," Orlando said, but he was smiling, and he stretched back out on the grass. "Well, what about Nutty? Do you think he really did all that stuff he's been telling everyone about?"

Bilbo gave that some thought. "Well, I'd say his batting average is about the same. I think if he gets up to bat ten times, he probably tells the truth once or twice."

"Oh, thanks, Bilbo," Nutty said. "What a great bunch of friends I've got." And Nutty really was irritated. He knew that he probably ought to take Bilbo's insult as well as Orlando had, but he couldn't. Everyone knew that Orlando exaggerated everything. But now Bilbo was implying that Nutty was out-and-out lying.

Richie was stuffing some cellophane wrappers back into his lunch sack. He wadded the sack up and then got up and walked over to a garbage can and dropped it in. "Well, I'll tell you, Nutty," he said, as he came back, "you have been laying it on pretty thick lately. At first we just thought it was funny and kind of stupid, but we're getting tired of it now."

"I guess there's no chance that you guys are a little jealous, huh?"

"Jealous of having Mindy hanging all over you?" Orlando said with disgust. "Jealous of wearing those sissy clothes to school every day?"

All the guys were looking quite satisfied with themselves, but it was Lance who bothered Nutty the most. He was watching Nutty, smiling a little more than usual. "What are you grinning about?" Nutty said.

"Grinning? I'm not grinning."

"What's with all you guys? You say I'm exaggerating. What about you? I do a little part in a movie and get a few new clothes, and all of a sudden you start treating me like I'm not even the same guy anymore."

107

"Come on, Nutty," Orlando said. He rolled over onto his back. "Take a look at reality. We're your best friends. Someone's got to tell you when you're acting like a geek."

"I'm not a geek. Don't call me that again."

"Okay, okay. How about jerk? Does that fit any better?"

All the guys laughed. Nutty didn't. But he wanted to. He also wanted to go home and change clothes and toss the shades in a dumpster somewhere. But he was in too deep. He didn't know how to get out of this whole mess.

The mess didn't go away, but the big night finally did come: the night of Nutty's movie. Mom and Dad were excited. Susie was purple with jealousy, but she wasn't missing it. Nutty was the only one not excited. He knew the moment of truth had come.

Nutty didn't really know exactly what the movie was about or where his scene fit into the story. But as it turned out, he didn't have to wait long. In fact, if he had blinked, he might have missed it. Somebody had edited most of the scene, and all that was left was one line. Only twenty minutes or so into the film, Harry— or, actually, the character he played—stopped his car and walked over to a farm. With the camera squarely on his face, he asked for directions. And then a bumpkin of a boy appeared on the screen and said, "Shucks, Mister, I don't think you can get there from here."

And he was gone. The red plaid shirt and the overalls, the straw hat—they were all there. Nutty had seen it but had not exactly recognized himself until the shot had disappeared from the screen. The other lines, the ones that came before, the directions and instructions—all that was gone. There had only been that one shot, the one line, and Harry had gone back to his car, shaking his head.

Nutty's parents seemed to miss it for a moment. And then Susie squealed and rolled over on her back. She began laughing hysterically. Nutty had tried to prepare her and his folks, but nothing quite excused the stupidity of what had appeared and passed away so quickly. The stupid look on his face, the stupid clothes, the stupid line—it was all so completely . . . stupid.

Susie was having fits, rolling around, grasping her sides. "Movie star. Movie star," she kept saying between gasps. And finally she managed to add, "What a movie star!"

Dad was stunned. He turned and stared at Nutty. Nutty could see that he didn't want to believe it.

"Was that it?" Mom finally said.

"They cut most of it," Nutty said, and he shrugged. He was trying to think of what he could do. Move away? Have plastic surgery done? Never leave his house again? Claim it was someone else? Kill William?

Dad got up from his chair and hurried to the TV. He flipped the VCR off "record" and then hit the reverse button. He backed it up a little too much at first and had to fast-forward. And then Nutty was there and gone again. That was when Nutty noticed that he sounded like a kid who appears in a school play and spouts off a memorized line.

Mr. Nutsell turned and looked at Nutty, the wonder still in his eyes. "You flew to Hollywood to do that?"

"It was just Burbank," Nutty said, without the slightest idea what he meant.

"They had to get someone from Warrensburg, Missouri, to say one sentence?"

"They cut the rest, Dad. I don't know why."

"I think I do," Dad said. "They just didn't cut it quite enough."

Susie was crying now. The laughter had been too intense and had somehow changed into joyous crying. "I've never been so happy in my whole life," she said. Nutty couldn't even work up enough strength to get mad at her.

"Honey, what will we tell people?" Mom asked. "All our friends were watching."

"I told you, Mom. I said it was just a dumb little part. I even told you what I said and everything."

"Oh, honey, I know, but . . . "

Dad tried, too, but neither one could find the words they were looking for.

Susie helped. "It was the stupidest thing that was ever on television."

Nutty thought that was the cruelest thing he had ever heard anyone say and that it was true. He slid deep into the couch he was sitting on and wished he could be swallowed up in the padding. It took him a little while to realize that the phone was ringing.

"You're going to have to get that, Freddie. I can't," Dad said, even though he was sitting next to the phone.

Nutty took his time. He thought that if he took long

enough, the ringing would stop. But on and on it went, and finally Nutty picked it up. "Yeah?" he said, trying to sound hostile, hoping to head off any smart remarks.

But all he heard was laughing. It was like Susie's, wild and joyous, but it was deeper. Nutty knew the voice, even though the caller never got any words out. "Orlando, you're not funny," Nutty said, and he hung up the phone.

"We could sell our house and move to another town," Dad was saying to Mom. "But I work here. I don't see how I can give everything up."

Nutty looked at his mother. He expected her to defend him. "Oh, Fred, it isn't that bad," she said. "I think if we drop out of the bridge club and just don't go anywhere for a few months, we'll be all right. It's bound to blow over in time." But then she added, "Oh, Fred, just think of how many people we told."

Nutty decided to go to his room. Susie was still sobbing, still holding her sides, and in a kind of ecstasy, saying over and over, "He's ruined forever. He's ruined forever."

"Oh, Susie, can you wait until tomorrow?"

"What?"

"I left my dirty gym socks at school. Is it all right if we wait until tomorrow to stuff them in your mouth?"

But she couldn't stop laughing long enough to think of an insult. Nutty was already long gone anyway. He thought maybe he'd just get under his bed and stay there until a hundred years had gone by.

Chapter 13

By morning Nutty's parents were saying that
they had to deal with "this thing" with all the
pride they could muster. They would just have to hold
their heads high. Nutty said he didn't want to go to
school, but Dad said, "I know, son. I don't blame you.
Your mother and I would rather not have to go to work
today either. But we're going to do it. And in a day or
two we're going to plug the phones back in. We're not
going to let this thing destroy us." He patted Nutty on
the shoulder a couple of times. "And remember, some
of it wasn't your fault."

Susie started to giggle, just gently, but Dad demanded she stop. "How you can take joy in something...like this...is beyond me, Susie. It's a family
tragedy, and I will not have you laughing about it."

She put her hands over her mouth, but Nutty could
see that her eyes were still laughing.

But Nutty didn't really care all that much. He would

have to feel a whole lot better than he did right now before he cared about anything.

It was in that spirit that he walked into the school building that morning. He had put on his old clothes—T-shirt and jeans with a hole in the knee—and left his shades home. But he had decided to take all the abuse and say not one word. No one could take pleasure in hurting a guy who didn't fight back—at least not for more than a month or two.

So Nutty walked up the sidewalk and stepped through the door, knowing exactly what to expect. There was the little pack of girls right where they would naturally be. He looked straight at them and surrendered.

"The star is here," Mindy announced, and everyone laughed.

Nutty kept his face blank, didn't say a word, didn't even act as though he had heard anything.

One of the girls did an imitation in a stiff, unnatural, but stupid voice. "Shucks, mister, I don't think you can get there from here." And then everyone picked it up, finally repeating the words in unison. Kids were gathering from everywhere, and Nutty could see that every single one had seen it.

"We had a party at Carrie's house. We taped it, and we watched it fifty times," Mindy said. She gestured at the group, implying that everyone had been there. "It was the funniest thing we've ever seen."

Mindy sounded a whole lot like Susie. Nutty had always known that she did not like him. It must have been a strain for her these last couple of weeks.

"Maybe next time you can play a clown. You could just look stupid—which you're good at—but not have to say anything."

Nutty was deciding that he was not so good at taking abuse as he had thought. He probably would have thrown some comeback at Mindy. He just couldn't think of one. He was about to push on through the little crowd and head to class when Mrs. Smiley came through the front doors and came over and put her arm around his shoulders. "Girls, please," she said. "Don't tease the poor guy. I know he's absolutely humiliated without your adding to his pain."

"I feel so very, very sorry for you, Nutty," Mrs. Smiley said. "If there's anything I can do to help, please let me know."

That was it. Nutty headed down the hall, almost trampling a couple of girls who didn't move fast enough to get out of his way. And then he heard someone say, "Great job, Nutty."

This got a big laugh, of course, but Nutty stopped long enough to look back. He was confused. He recognized Lance's voice; what he didn't hear was any humor, any teasing. The guy seemed to mean it.

"Really," Lance said. "Every actor has to break in somehow. And he has to do whatever the director tells him to do. Maybe it wasn't much of a part, but how many people can say they were in a movie?"

"He was terrible," Mindy said.

"Hey, they asked him to play a dumb hick," Lance said. "He played it perfectly. Did you see that stupid look on his face?"

Nutty still wasn't sure. He thought Lance was just finding a way to put him down. But if that's what he was up to, his method was very subtle.

"Yeah, he looked stupid all right," one of the girls said, and all the kids laughed.

"That's right. And that's what he was instructed to do. It was a comedy. And he was playing a funny character. You were supposed to laugh, and you did. So he did what he set out to do."

"We didn't laugh because he was funny. We laughed because he did a lousy job."

Lance stepped up next to Nutty. "Did the director tell you how to deliver your lines?"

Nutty sort of shrugged, and then he nodded.

"Well, see. Nutty just played the role the way they asked him to play it. That's what actors do. All the great actors have to do a few bit parts before they finally hit the big time. Someday you'll all be saying, 'I knew Parker back when he played that first silly little part on TV.'"

No one was laughing now. Mindy was still trying to smile, but she was losing her confidence.

"Remember, he's been telling you for weeks that he thought the part was stupid. I don't see why anyone's surprised."

Nutty finally found himself wanting to explain. "The part I actually filmed was a lot longer than that. For some reason they cut most of the lines."

"That always happens," Lance said. "They end up with a movie that's too long. And they won't cut any of their commercials, so they have to cut the movie

115

itself. That's just part of show business."

Mrs. Smiley stepped back over to Nutty. "That's right, Nutty. I wouldn't feel bad about it. I still think you're going to get your chance to do some big things."

The moment was at a balance. Nutty could see Mindy holding ground, wondering which way to go. "Well," she finally said, "you'll have to admit it was pretty stupid."

"Mega-stupid," Nutty said.

"But maybe your next part will be better."

"At least he got to go to Hollywood," Zoie said.

"And meet Kirk Cameron."

Nutty felt the change, even saw it in the kids' faces. He looked at Lance, who gave him a nod. "Maybe you ought to do some acting," Nutty said.

"Me? Nah. I don't think so." And there was that strange little smile. What was this guy up to? Nutty owed him a lot right now, and yet there was something . . . something he could never get hold of. Maybe Lance had really been making fun of him the whole time, and he was having fun because he was the only one in on the private joke. But everyone had stopped laughing, and somewhere in the crowd Nutty heard a girl talking about him, calling him Parker. He was Parker again. Nutty wasn't sure that in the long run he wouldn't have been better off going back to the humiliation, but for the moment Parker was welcome.

Nutty found himself saying, "Thanks, Lance."

"Hey, don't thank me. I didn't do anything."

Mrs. Smiley said it was time to get to class, and Nutty headed for the room, but when he realized that Lance was walking with him, he stopped at his locker. He just wanted to shake the guy loose long enough to think the whole thing over. As the kids moved on past, Nutty was sort of relieved to be out of the center of things. But just as he opened his locker, he realized that someone had stopped next to him. He turned and looked at Sarah.

"So how are you doing?" she said. She hadn't been there when all the teasing had been going on. She had apparently just come into the school. Nutty was interested that she didn't start making fun of him.

"I don't know. They cut most of my part, and what was left was really stupid."

"Well, you couldn't help that. The whole movie was bad."

That was true. Nutty hadn't watched anything past his own part, but the opening had been terrible. For some reason, he felt better remembering that.

"Are you going to get some more parts, do you think?"

Nutty knew what he had been telling everyone, but he was in no mood to talk that way today. "I don't think so. I don't think I like acting. I'm not any good at it."

"You haven't really acted before. Maybe you ought to take some lessons."

"I don't think so."

"So don't you want to be a movie star?"

"Do you think I should?"

She leaned against the locker next to his, and she smiled. "It'd be pretty neat, I guess," she said. "But I just think ... "

"What?"

"Nothing."

"No. Come on. Tell me."

She was blushing. "Well, you could do a lot of things. For one thing, you could be a star basketball player, if you wanted to. But . . . "

"But what?"

"I think whatever you do, you should just stay yourself. And not act so . . . different."

Nutty nodded. Now she was thinking the same thing he was; he just hadn't known that's what he was thinking until she said the words. Which was all very strange. He also noticed that she was making those dimples he liked so much. He was almost feeling like a human again.

"Hey, Nutty."

Nutty didn't have to look. He knew Orlando's voice. He grabbed a book from his locker and pushed the door shut. He was getting out of there.

"Nutty, do you think you might win the Academy Award for your performance?"

"It was television. You get an Emmy for that," Richie said, and both boys laughed. Nutty glanced back and saw that Bilbo was there, too.

"Don't tease him, you guys," Sarah said. "He feels lousy enough as it is."

Orlando cracked up. "Oooooh, Sarah. Only a woman in love could stick with a guy after that movie."

That was all for Sarah. She took off, walking fast. Nutty told Orlando to shut his mouth, and then he walked away himself.

"But Parker," Orlando said, "I wanted your autograph."

Nutty stopped and spun around. "Look, you guys, I'm finished with acting. And I won't be stupid around school anymore. I won't wear geeky clothes and shades and all that stuff. If Mindy treats me like she likes me, I'll spit on my hand and pat her on the cheek—the way I did that one time. I'm back to myself. Honest."

"So who liked you the way you were?"

"You did," Nutty said, and he waited until Orlando came closer, and he slugged him on the shoulder.

Chapter 14

Nutty went in and sat down. All he wanted to do was to blend in for a while. He'd never before been so tired of being looked at. He no more than slipped into his desk, however, before Mindy turned around and stared right at him. "What do you want, Mindy?" Nutty said, but he didn't dare tell her to leave him alone; he didn't need any more problems with her.

"I'm trying to decide what to do," she said.

"What are you talking about?"

"Do you really think you'll get into some more movies and be a big star and everything?"

"I don't know." But then Nutty decided to go ahead and tell the truth. He was tired of all this lying. "I really doubt it."

"Yeah, me too." She held her lips very tight and squinted. Nutty figured she must be trying to think—which wasn't really a natural demand to put upon herself. "But if you just happened to make it, and I'd been treating you bad and you hated me, I'd kick myself forever."

"Mindy, let's face it, I don't like you much. And you don't like me."

"I know." She did some lip and eye tightening again. "The worst thing would be if I'm nice to you, and then you never make it in the movies. Then I'd hate myself."

Nutty sort of laughed. "That would be bad," he said. "Maybe we could just sort of avoid each other."

But Mindy saw no humor in any of this. "No, that's just as bad. If you're a big star, I want to be on your good side."

"I guess you could try to play up to me—just in case. But I don't think it will work. I probably won't like you either way."

"Yeah...but if I worked at it for a year or two, I could probably bring you around. It's just that I'll be miserable the whole time, and then, if you end up like I think you will—just a big nothing—"

"You'd never forgive yourself."

"Right."

Nutty had a very good laugh this time; Mindy seemed confused. But Mrs. Smiley was telling her to turn around now, so the great question was never really resolved. But Nutty did notice something strange during the recess. Mindy spent much of the time, along with some other girls, talking to Lance. Nutty had a hunch that she was getting Lance's opinion on her problem, but he wasn't sure he cared very much. He was occupied with trying to be a regular guy—just playing a little touch football and not doing one thing to call any attention to himself.

But when lunchtime came, something strange happened. Lance came over to Nutty and said, "Can I talk to you?"

"Sure."

"I mean alone—for a little while."

"All right."

"Let's go get our lunches. We can go out and eat in front of the school. The other guys will be out back."

Nutty was not too excited about the idea, but he figured he owed Lance something after what Lance had done for him that morning. He just wasn't sure he trusted the guy.

Nutty noticed that Mindy was craning her neck to hear what he and Lance were saying, but he didn't care if she heard. He did sort of wonder what she was telling the other girls as he and Lance left the room, but he didn't worry about it. The boys walked down the hall to their lockers and got their lunches. Somehow it never registered with him that the girls didn't come down the hallway, the way they normally did.

As soon as Nutty and Lance were outside, Nutty said, "Thanks for helping me out this morning. You saved my life."

"No big deal," Lance said. Nutty wasn't sure how to take that. "The important thing is, it worked." Nutty was even less sure what that meant.

The boys sat down on the grass near the shrubs along the front of the building. Nutty got out his peanut butter sandwich. The thought crossed his mind that he really did have to do something about the cafeteria. He hated these sack lunches. "So how come you decided to help me out? I haven't done anything for you."

"I don't know, Nutty. I guess I just want to be your friend." But there was that little smile again, the one that always made Nutty think that the guy didn't mean what he was saying.

"Oh, yeah? How come you want to be my friend?" Nutty asked.

"Well, I found out that my Dad's not going to be here very long. We'll probably be moving in a couple of months. But I need someone to hang around with this summer. You're about the coolest guy I've met here."

"You said all that stuff just so we could be friends?"

"Oh, no. I don't mean that exactly. Everything I said was true, wasn't it? You still plan to be in movies, don't you? Isn't William still working on that?"

"How do you know about William?"

"Everyone knows about William. He's the guy who got you to Hollywood. The way I hear it, he thinks up everything for you."

Nutty was pretty sure Lance had just given him a shot. But the guy never came straight out with anything.

"You are still going to be in some movies, aren't you?"

"I don't know. I don't think I want to."

"Really?"

Nutty had the feeling that Lance was trying to get him to say something. He wasn't about to do it. "I'll just have to see how it goes."

"Let me give you some advice, Nutty. I've been to a

lot of different schools. I've learned a few things." Lance was peeling a banana, slowly and precisely, but he glanced up and smiled, or maybe he had never stopped smiling—just slightly. "If you want to be really popular, you ought to dump this William guy. He's hurting you more than helping you."

"Oh, is that right?" Nutty said. "And you know all about it, I guess."

"Yes, I think so. He did okay getting you in a movie, but he never should have told you to wear those clothes. And, especially, he shouldn't have told you to tell all those lies when you got back from California. That was a big mistake."

"What lies?"

"Come on, Nutty. You didn't meet Kirk Cameron. You didn't do half that stuff you've been telling everyone. You didn't have time. You know you were at the studio most of the time you were there, and the studio was way outside Hollywood."

Nutty wasn't talking. Lance might have helped him that morning, but the guy was not his friend, no matter what he said.

"Hey, it's not your fault," Lance said. "This William guy told you to say all that stuff, didn't he?"

"No, he didn't."

"Don't tell me it was your idea."

"Look, it wasn't anybody's idea. I was just embarrassed about that stupid part, so I wanted to make the trip sound as good as I could."

"I guess you didn't see Kirk Cameron at all, did you?"

"Well, I—"

"Don't start with me, Nutty. I know you didn't see him."

"No, I didn't. All right? I didn't see Eddie Murphy either. I didn't even see Hollywood. I spent the whole time in Burbank. But don't tell anybody, okay?"

"Hey, don't worry about me. Why would I want to tell anyone?" Lance ate the last of his banana, and then he searched inside the sack and found a package of Twinkies. "I hate these things. Do you want them?"

Nutty loved Twinkies, but he didn't take them. He wasn't taking anything from Lance. And he already wished he hadn't admitted anything. He decided to get away from Lance as soon as he could.

"Look, Nutty, it's none of my business. I just think you ought to know that people are on to you. I'd lay off all those stories."

"I already have."

"Do you think Sarah knows you've been lying?"

"Look, Lance—"

"Hey, I just mean, if you're going with her, and she finds out you've been lying, she's going to dump you."

"Who said I'm going with her?"

"Everyone. You do like her, don't you?"

"Lance, I don't know what you're trying to do. How come you're asking me so many questions?"

"Hey, I'm just trying to give you some advice. For all I know, you don't even like Sarah. Are you really going with her or not?"

"No, Lance. I'm not going with anyone. I'm in the fifth grade, for crying out loud."

"Hey, fifth graders go together. All the time."

"Well, I don't." Nutty grabbed his sack, and then he got up.

"Okay, fine." Lance didn't stand up. He sat with his legs crossed and looked up at Nutty. "I think you're playing it smart. If you get in a movie, you might meet somebody really hot. Sarah would be nothing compared to some of those actresses they have out in Hollywood."

"Lance, shut up, okay? Everything you say makes me mad."

"Why? I don't get that. You and I both know that Sarah can't compare to some of those movie stars. She's kind of cute, but not like—"

"Hey—she's a lot more than 'kind of cute.' Okay?"

"Do you really think so?"

"Yeah, really."

"Come on—tell the truth. If you were in a movie, and you had a chance to give one of those big, long, lingering kisses to somebody, you wouldn't choose little ol' Sarah from Warrensburg. You'd pick some movie star."

"Look, Lance, I don't give anybody any long, lingering kisses."

"But if you did, you'd pick Sarah Montag?"

"Why not? She's as good-looking as any movie star. And she's probably a heck of a lot nicer."

And that's when the giggling started. In the bushes. The whole bunch of them—the fifth-grade girls—were behind the shrubbery, next to the school. It took Nutty about one full second to realize they had heard every word of what he and Lance had said.

"You girls are rotten," Nutty yelled. "What are you doing back there?"

"Yeah, right," Mindy said, as she pushed her way out through some junipers. "You're a fine one to talk."

But another girl, still in the bushes, was saying, "Hey, Nutty, here she is back here. Come on in and get that long, lingering kiss you were talking about."

Nutty died. When he had fallen through the ceiling, he thought he had dropped as low as he could go. When he saw himself on TV, he was sure that he had hit a new bottom, that nothing worse could ever happen to him. But this was it—the bargain basement of all embarrassments. If he lived forever, these girls would never let him live this one down.

Mindy had apparently made up her mind about Nutty's future. She told him he was a big liar and a big jerk, and then she started listing his many character faults. Most of the girls added their own little details to Mindy's description. But when they started thanking Lance for letting them listen, and for getting Nutty to admit the truth, Nutty thought about jumping on the guy and doing a manual heart transplant. The only trouble was, he was much more angry with himself than he was with Lance. He realized what he wanted most was just to get away from everyone.

As he turned to go, however, the attention came back to him. "So you didn't meet Kirk Cameron, huh, Nutty? My, my, you've been telling stories."

Nutty kept going. He wanted to move to South America or Australia, maybe the Antarctic. He wanted to cover up his face and never show it again anywhere. But none of that was possible, so he walked back to the classroom and sat down, all by himself. He tried to hypnotize himself, to tell himself that he was in another place and could hear nothing, feel nothing. He almost had himself convinced until the girls came through the door.

"Hey, Parker, that was sure a short movie career."

"What else did you lie about? Did you even go to California?"

"Hey, hot lips, are you ready to plant one on Sarah now?"

"Yeah, Nutty, if you want to give her one of those big, movie star kisses, what are you waiting for?"

Richie, Bilbo, and Orlando had come in. "What's this?" Orlando said.

Nutty wasn't talking. He was trying to think how long it would take to live this one down. Maybe if he lived in another state, didn't ever see a single person from the lab school, had plastic surgery, changed his name, and suffered from amnesia—maybe then, at least after fifty years, he would be able to put all this behind him.

"Oh, haven't you heard, Orlando?" Mindy said. "Nutty just admitted that he didn't meet Kirk Cameron. He didn't even go to Hollywood."

"Yeah," Zoie said, "and he also said he wants to give Sarah a big, long kiss on the lips."

I wonder when the first people will start moving to Mars? Nutty thought. Whenever it is, I'm getting my name on the list.

Chapter 15

Nutty hardly moved all afternoon. He sat stiff as a board in his seat, staring ahead. When Mrs. Smiley noticed and asked him whether he was all right, he said, "Yeah, I'm okay."

But Mindy said, "He's had a bad day," and everyone in the class started laughing. By now, everyone knew the whole story.

Mrs. Smiley left Nutty alone after that. When afternoon recess came, Nutty stayed in his seat. And when Mrs. Smiley asked what he was doing, he said, "I'd just like to stay here, if it's all right." She didn't even probe. She just told him that would be fine, and she left him alone.

Nutty was waiting for one thing only at this point: the end of the school day. When it came, he got up and got out as quickly as he could. A few little insults followed him down the hallway, but almost everyone stopped at their lockers, and he just kept going. He got outside fast, and he headed down the street away from the school. He was working on a plan. Dad was still embarrassed about the movie; he had said something about moving. Nutty was thinking now might be the time to get Dad to take a serious look at that possibility. Maybe he could get William to go into the real-estate business and find his dad an offer he couldn't refuse. Maybe he could—

"Nutty. Wait."

Nutty slowed but didn't stop. He knew the voice, but he didn't think he could face the face.

"Wait a minute. I want to talk to you."

He came to a stop, but he didn't turn around. How could he ever look at her again? But she was coming up behind him, and in another second she passed him and turned around.

Nutty felt himself turn red from his toenails to the end of each hair on his head. Instant sweat. One thing he had done all afternoon was never look at her, but now, here she was right in front of him. He looked to the side of her, focused in on a distant house. But he did get some words out. "I'm sorry," he said, in a sort of gulp.

"For what?"

Nutty wasn't going to try to put that many words together. He just made a wide motion with his hand, as if to say, "Everything." But he did take a glance at her, and she didn't look mad. She looked sort of worried or concerned or . . . something.

"You don't have to be so embarrassed," she said.

Nutty took another glance at her. He thought maybe she had lost her mind.

"Lots of kids do something and then make it a bigger deal than it really was."

Nutty looked down at the sidewalk. "I made nothing into a big deal."

"It's still the same thing."

Nutty let his breath flow out. He had no idea what to say. There was no way he could just forget the whole thing. "They're going to tease me forever," he said.

"Not really. Some of the girls are already starting to feel sorry for you. Carrie said that what Lance did to you was worse than what you did."

That didn't exactly help, except that he could tell that Sarah was on his side. "Sarah, I didn't mean it the way it sounded...about the kissing. Lance just kept saying that movie stars would be better. I only meant that they wouldn't. I didn't mean I wanted to kiss you. Really, I don't want to."

Nutty hadn't looked at her through all that, but when she didn't respond, he took another glance. She was sort of laughing, and she was sort of red, and he didn't know what any of that meant. "Thanks a lot," she said.

"Oh, I didn't mean...I mean, I think you're...you are, you know...cute...but I don't kiss people...or, I mean, girls. I don't want to...kiss anybody..."

"That's okay, Nutty. I don't want to kiss you either."

He nodded, relieved and maybe just a little disappointed.

But she wasn't talking, and he couldn't just stand there. "It's probably sort of gross," he said, but he was looking at her now, and he didn't really believe it.

"What is?"

"Kissing. I don't mean it would be gross to kiss you. It's probably just gross to kiss."

"I don't think so."

"You don't? Have you ever..."

"No. I just mean it probably isn't so gross. But I don't want to kiss. I don't mean that."

"Ever?" Suddenly Nutty was a little worried he had pushed the whole thing a little too far.

But this embarrassed her, and now the two of them were both staring at the ground. Nutty tried hard to think of something to say that would get him out of this whole conversation, but just as he was about to decide that no words would ever occur to him, he heard a distant voice—a deep, important-sounding voice that could belong to only one person. He turned around and saw William hurrying toward him, saying, "Nutty, Nutty, I have great news."

William strode up to them but then stopped and took a couple of long breaths before he tried to explain. "I've had the most amazing day. Matthiesen called me early this morning, and we've been in negotiation all day. I didn't even go to school."

"What are you talking about, William?" It wasn't at all like William to miss a day at his private school even though he knew more than his teachers did already.

"I've got a big contract for you. You're going to star in your own feature."

"No way, William. I've had enough of—"

"Nutty, I have no time for silly objections. I've got you some real bucks, a major part, and get this—the film will be shot here in Warrensburg. If I can work it

132

out with Dr. Dunlop, a lot of the scenes will be shot right in the lab school." William looked at Sarah. "There's a part for you, too, if you can do all right in the auditions. Matthiesen said he'd use some local talent for leads, where possible, and he can use all the kids in the fifth grade for extras."

"Why?" Sarah said, and she was obviously stunned.

"Why what?"

"Why here? Why the lab school?"

"Oh, that's the whole point. The director of that film Nutty did thinks that Nutty's great. He wants the whole movie to be full of real people—down-to-earth, rural, solid types."

"William," Nutty said, "that guy is nuts. He'll make another movie as bad as that one I was in before. He'll come in here and scream and shout and act crazy, and people will run him out of town. It won't work."

"Of course it will work. Granted, the movie may not be great, but you'll have enough money to go to any college you want to, and every one of your friends will make some bucks, too. The plan is to shoot the film this summer." He tucked his hands into his pockets and smiled with great satisfaction.

Nutty didn't know what to think. He had made up his mind never to act again. But William had him by the arm and was marching him back to the school. "I need to talk to Dunlop," he was saying.

"What's the movie about?" Sarah wanted to know.

"Who knows? He said something about a little farming community; that's all I know."

"This isn't a farming community, William."

"Yeah, well, it's close enough. They'll probably shoot some of the scenes in smaller towns around here."

When William reached the school, he spotted some of the fifth-grade girls. Nutty saw that they were just getting ready to start the teasing all over again when William said, "Girls, don't go away. I have the most exciting news you're going to hear—let's say, this year—but the truth is, it may be the most exciting news you'll ever hear in your lives. May I trust that you'll wait around until Nutty and I have talked to Dr. Dunlop for a few minutes?"

They were looking curious, but maybe a little doubtful. Mindy said, "William, don't act so important. I'm sure it's nothing that big."

But when Sarah said, "It's pretty big," in a voice alive with excitement, the girls said they would wait.

"See if you can spot Orlando and Bilbo and any of the other fellows," William said, and he walked on into the school, with Nutty following close behind.

Dr. Dunlop was just coming out of his office as William came walking in. Dunlop looked a little frightened when he said, "What is it this time?"

"Great news, sir," William said, and then he walked right past Dr. Dunlop into his office. "Step inside for just a moment, and let me explain."

Dr. Dunlop was not pleased, but he accepted the invitation—to come into his own office. He stood before William with his arms folded, and he looked down on him with his jaw set, obviously ready for the worst.

By the time William had explained everything, however, Dr. Dunlop had loosened up, and he was much more excited than he wanted to admit. He kept trying to sound skeptical, but Nutty could see he was as excited as the kids would be to think a movie would be shot right in his school. "Well, yes," he said. "I believe something of that sort is possible. We could work with a movie company. If the people from the company would contact me directly, I'm sure we can work something out."

"They're willing to pay two thousand dollars a day, sir. I already discussed that with them. And they need a person to play the role of the principal in the film. I told them you might be just the fellow."

Dr. Dunlop tried not to smile, but if William had been Little Red Riding Hood and he had been the big bad wolf, his eyes couldn't have been any bigger. "Yes, yes. That sounds quite interesting. We'll have to clear the whole matter with the university of course, and—"

"I can take care of that if you'd like. It's simply a matter of—"

"No, William. I'll take care of it."

"Then it's settled?"

"Well, probably. I still want someone to contact me directly." Dr. Dunlop pushed his hands down in his pockets, nodding seriously. "What sort of part is it, anyway?" The smile was sneaking back.

"I think the principal is supposed to be very hard-nosed, very strict. I don't know; maybe you won't be able to play a role like that. You're just not that type."

"Well, I could . . . give it a try."

Somewhere in the middle of all this, Nutty had gotten the first glimmering of an idea that was now taking shape very fast.

"Oh, William, didn't you mention that the movie people said something about the cafeteria in the school—the one in the movie?"

"Excuse me? I don't remember—"

"Yeah, you said that it's a very modern kind of school, where the kids eat pizza and hamburgers—the way kids do in the really up-to-date schools around the country."

Nutty saw the light go on in William's head. "Oh, oh. Yes, that's right. But I'm sure you do that. When I attended school here that wasn't the case, but I remember Dr. Dunlop promising some changes."

"Well, yes. We've been looking into that," Dr. Dunlop said.

"Good. Just be certain that's all in place right away. I believe the movie has a couple of cafeteria scenes. You'll need to be able to assure the movie producer that your people cook those kinds of dishes quite often. They wouldn't want some out-of-date sort of school for their film."

"Yes, well, I think that's easy enough to work out. It's something I've been in favor of all along. It's just taken a little time to get some of those things worked out."

"Well, good. It sounds like we're set. You just start practicing being very strict, walking around with a mean look on your face, that sort of thing. It will take a while, but you'll get the feel of it."

Dr. Dunlop promised it would be no problem, and William and Nutty left. Outside, they found most of the fifth graders. Sarah had resisted telling everyone what was going on. She let William break the news.

Nutty watched Mindy as William explained what was happening. The skeptical look left her face immediately. She was soon in ecstasy. "What sort of parts can we try out for?" she said. "Would I fit any of them?"

"There's a need for one girl to play Nutty's girlfriend," William said. "And there's another girl who will play a sort of villainess. She'll be a nasty thing—cause people trouble, smart mouth, all that sort of thing."

"Oh, that's perfect for me. I can play Parker's girlfriend."

"What about parts for guys?" Orlando wanted to know. "Is there a part for Nutty's best friend?"

"Yes." William nodded quietly. "I thought I might try out for that one. But Bilbo would be good too."

"What are you talking about? I've been his best friend forever."

"I'm better friends with him than you are," Richie said.

Zoie mumbled, "I've had a crush on him since second grade. I think I should be his girlfriend."

But a lot of girls disagreed.

Nutty couldn't believe it. He looked around at everyone. They were all going nuts. They were as excited as if they had just inherited a million dollars each, but they were already fighting over each other's money— like a pride of lions going after the same meat. And then he heard Mindy say, "I've got to get a whole new wardrobe."

Orlando picked up the thought. "Hey, yeah, Nutty, where did you get those clothes? And I need some shades."

"What do you need new clothes for?"

"Come on. Be serious. If a guy's going to be a movie star, he has to have a certain look. You know that as well as anyone." He was sort of laughing, but Nutty thought he was at least half serious.

"Do we have to do the film here?" Mindy asked. "Why can't we shoot some of it in Hollywood? I'd like to meet Kirk and some of your other friends."

"Mindy, I didn't—"

"Well, that's all right. If we start here, there's no stopping us. We'll spend plenty of time in Hollywood." She gave her hair a flip. "I think I'll have my hair lightened a little. Don't you think it would look good that way, Parker?"

Nutty just shook his head. He couldn't believe any of this. But William was tapping his shoulder, and Nutty bent down. William whispered in his ear, "I don't know how we're going to break it to them, but they all have to wear bib overalls and straw hats."

The two boys began to laugh, and the more they pictured it, the more they cracked up. Nutty had to lean on William for strength. "I can just see Mindy with long braids and freckles on her nose," William said.

"Yeah, and a missing tooth," Nutty said. But then he had another thought. "Hey, is there any kissing in this movie?"

"I really don't know. Are you hoping there is, or that there isn't?"

Nutty looked over at Sarah, thought about that for a moment, and then said, "Both, I think."